INTERNATIONAL

# THE
# ASSIGNMENT

BOOKS BY FRIEDRICH DÜRRENMATT

*The Visit*
*The Physicists*

# FRIEDRICH DÜRRENMATT

# THE ASSIGNMENT

*Or*
*On the Observing of the Observer*
*of the Observers*

Translated from the German
by Joel Agee

VINTAGE INTERNATIONAL

*Vintage Books*
*A Division of Random House, Inc.*
*New York*

First Vintage International Edition, June 1989

Translation copyright © 1988 by Joel Agee

Library of Congress Cataloging-in-Publication Data
Dürrenmatt, Friedrich.
[Auftrag. English]
The assignment, or, On the observing of the observer of
the observers / Friedrich Dürrenmatt ; translated from
the German by Joel Agee— 1st Vintage international ed.
    p.   cm.—(Vintage international)
Translation of: Der Auftrag.
ISBN 0-679-72233-5 : $7.95
I. Title.   II. Title: Assignment.   III. Title: On the
observing of the observer of the observers.
[PT2607.U493A9413      1989]
833'.914—dc 19                               88-40368
                                                              CIP

Manufactured in the United States of America
10  9  8  7  6  5  4  3  2  1

What will come? What will the future bring? I do not know. I have no presentiment. When a spider plunges from a fixed point to its consequences, it always sees before it an empty space where it can never set foot, no matter how it wriggles. It is that way with me: before me always an empty space; what drives me forward is a consequence that lies behind me. This life is perverse and frightful, it is unbearable.

—Søren Kierkegaard

# THE
# ASSIGNMENT

**|||** **1** **|||** When Otto von Lambert was informed by the police that his wife Tina had been found dead and violated at the foot of the Al-Hakim ruin, and that the crime was as yet unsolved, the psychiatrist, well known for his book on terrorism, had the corpse transported by helicopter across the Mediterranean, suspended in its coffin by ropes from the bottom of the plane, so that it trailed after it slightly, over vast stretches of sunlit land, through shreds of clouds, across the Alps in a snowstorm, and later through rain showers, until it was gently reeled down into an open grave surrounded by a mourning party, and covered with earth, whereupon von Lambert, who had noticed that

3

F., too, had filmed the event, briefly scrutinized her and, closing his umbrella despite the rain, demanded that she and her team visit him that same evening, since he had an assignment for her that could not be delayed.

‖ 2 ‖ F., well known for her film portraits, who had resolved to explore new paths and was pursuing the still vague idea of creating a total portrait, namely a portrait of our planet, by combining random scenes into a whole, which was the reason why she had filmed the strange burial, stood staring after the massively built man, von Lambert, who, drenched and unshaven, had accosted her, and had turned his back on her without greeting, and she decided only after some hesitation to do what he had asked, for she had an unpleasant feeling that something was not right, and that besides, she was running the danger of being drawn into a story that would deflect her from

5

her plans, so that it was with a feeling of repugnance that she arrived with her crew at the psychiatrist's house, impelled by curiosity about the nature of his offer but determined to refuse whatever it was.

||| 3 ||| Von Lambert received her in his studio, demanded to be immediately filmed, willingly submitted to all the preparations, and then, sitting behind his desk, explained to the running camera that he was guilty of his wife's death because he had always treated the heavily depressed woman as a case instead of as a person, until she had accidentally discovered his notes on her sickness and, according to the maid, left the house straight away, a red fur coat thrown over her denim suit, clutching her pocketbook, after which he had not heard from her at all, but neither had he undertaken to learn her whereabouts, if only to grant her whatever freedom she desired, or, on the other hand,

7

should she discover his investigations, to spare her the feeling that she was being watched from a distance, but now that she had come to such a terrible end he was forced to recognize his guilt not only in having treated her with the cool scrutiny prescribed by psychoanalytic practice but also in having failed to investigate her disappearance, he regarded it as his duty to find out the truth, and beyond that, to make it available to science, since his wife's fate had brought him up against the limits of his profession, but since he was a physical wreck and not capable of taking the trip himself, he was giving her, F., the assignment of reconstructing the murder (of which he as her doctor was the primary cause, the actual perpetrator being but an accidental factor) at the apparent scene of the crime, of recording whatever was there to be recorded, so that the results could be shown at psychoanalytic conferences and presented to the state prosecutor's office, since, being guilty, he, like any criminal, had lost the right to keep his failure secret, and having said this, he handed her a check for a considerable sum of money, several photographs of the murdered woman, her journal, and his notes, whereupon F., much to the surprise of her crew, accepted the assignment.

||| **4** ||| After leaving the psychiatrist's house, F. refused to answer her cameraman's question as to the meaning of all this nonsense, spent most of the night perusing the journal and the doctor's notes, and, after a brief sleep, still in bed, made arrangements with a travel agency for the flight to M., drove into town, bought several newspapers with pictures of the strange funeral and the dead woman on their front pages, and, before checking a hastily scribbled address she had found in the journal, went to an Italian restaurant for breakfast, where she encountered the logician D., whose lectures at the university were attended by two or three students—an eccentric and sharp-witted man

9

of whom no one could tell whether he was unfit for life or merely pretended to be helpless, who expounded his logical problems to anyone who joined him at his table in the always crowded restaurant, and this in such a confused and thoroughgoing manner that no one was able to understand him, not F. either, though she found him amusing, liked him, and often told him about her plans, as she did now, mentioning first the peculiar assignment she had been given, and going on to talk about the dead woman's journal, as if to herself, unconscious of her interlocutor, so preoccupied was she by that densely filled notebook: never, she said, never in her life had she read a similar description of a person, Tina von Lambert had portrayed her husband as a monster, but gradually, not immediately, virtually peeling off pieces of him, facet by facet, examining each one separately, as if under a microscope, constantly narrowing and magnifying the focus and sharpening the light, page after page about his eating habits, page after page about the way he picked his teeth, page after page about how and where he scratched himself, page after page about his coughing or sneezing or clearing his throat or smacking his lips, his involuntary movements, gestures, twitches, idiosyncrasies more or less common to most people, but described in such a way that she, F., had a hard time contemplating the subject of food now, and if she had not touched her breakfast yet, it was only because she could not help imagining that she herself was disgusting to look at while eating, for it was impossible to eat aesthetically, and reading this journal was like being immersed in a cloud of pure observations gradually condensing into a lump of hate and revulsion, or like reading a film script for a documentary of every human being, as if every person, if he or she were filmed in this manner, would turn into a von Lambert as he was described by this woman, all individuality crushed out by such ruthless observation, while F.'s own impression of the psychiatrist had been one of a fanatic who was beginning to doubt his cause, extraordinarily childlike and helpless in a way that reminded her of many scientists, a man who had always believed and still believed that he loved his wife, and to whom it had never occurred that it was all too easy to imagine that one loved someone, and that basically one loved only oneself, but even before meeting him, the spectacular funeral had made her suspect that its purpose was to cover up his hurt pride, why not, and as for the assignment to hunt for the circumstances of her death, he was probably trying, albeit unconsciously, to build a monument to himself, and if Tina's description of her husband was grotesque in its exaggeration and excessive concreteness, von Lambert's notes were equally grotesque in their abstraction, they weren't observations at all but literally an abstracting of her humanity, defining depression as a psychosomatic phenomenon resulting from insight into the meaninglessness of existence, which is inherent in existence itself, since the meaning of existence *is* existence, which insight, once accepted and affirmed, makes existence unbearable, so that Tina's insight into that insight *was* the depression, and so forth, this sort of idiocy page after page, which made it seem inconceivable to her that Tina had fled as a result of having read these pages, as von Lambert apparently suspected, even though two of her journal entries ended with the doubly underlined sentence: "I am being watched," a statement for which F. had a different interpretation, namely that Tina had found out that von Lambert had read her journal, obviously a much more shattering discovery than von Lambert's notes could have been, since, for one who secretly hates and suddenly learns that the hated one knows it, there could be no other way out than to flee, at which point F. ended her comments with the remark that something about this story was not right, there still was the riddle of what could have driven Tina into the desert, it was all beginning to make her feel like one of those probes they shoot out into space in the hope that they will transmit back to the earth information about its still unknown composition.

‖ 5 ‖ D. had listened to F.'s report and absently ordered a glass of wine, even though it was just eleven o'clock, gulped it down with an equally absent air, ordered a second glass, and remarked that he was still pondering the useless problem of whether the law of identity $A = A$ was correct, since it posited two identical A's, while actually there could only be one A identical with itself, and anyway, applied to reality it was quite meaningless, since there was no self-identical person anywhere, because everyone was subject to time and was therefore, strictly speaking, a different person at every moment, which was why he, D., sometimes had the impression that he was a different person each morning, as if a different self had replaced his previous self and were using his brain and consequently his memory, making him all the more glad that he was a logician, for logic was beyond all reality and removed from every sort of existential mishap, and so he would like to respond to the story she had told him but could only do so in very general terms: good old von Lambert had no doubt experienced a shock, not as a husband, though, but as a psychiatrist whose patient has fled, and now he was turning his human failing into a failure of psychiatry, and the psychiatrist was left standing like a jailer without prisoners, bereft of his subject, and what he was calling his fault was this lack, what he wanted from F. was merely the missing document for his documentation, by trying to know what he could never understand, he was hoping to bring the dead woman back into captivity, and the whole thing would be perfect material for a comedy if it didn't contain a problem that had been troubling him, D., for a long time, a logical problem loosely involving a mirror telescope he had installed in his house in the mountains, an unwieldy thing that he occasionally pointed at a cliff from which he was being observed by people with field glasses, with the effect that, as soon as the people observing him through their field glasses realized that he was observing them through his telescope, they would retreat in a hurry, an empirical confirmation, in short, of the logical conclusion that anything observed requires the presence of an observer, who, if he is observed by what he is observing, himself becomes an object of observation, a banal logical interaction, which, however, transposed into reality, had a destabilizing effect, for the people observing him and discovering that he was observing them through a mirror telescope felt caught in the act, and since being caught in the act produces embarrassment and embarrassment frequently leads to aggression, more than one of these people, after retreating in haste, had come back to throw rocks at his house as soon as he had dismantled the telescope, a dialectical process, said D., that was symptomatic of our time, when everyone observed and felt observed by everyone else, so that a very suitable definition of contemporary man might be that he is man under observation— observed by the state, for one, with more and more sophisticated methods, while man makes more and more desperate attempts to escape being observed, which in turn renders man increasingly suspect in the eyes of the state and the state even more suspect in the eyes of man; similarly each state observes and feels observed by all the other states, and man, on another plane, is busy observing nature as never before, inventing more and more subtle instruments for this purpose, cameras, telescopes, stereoscopes, radio telescopes, X-ray telescopes, microscopes, synchrotrons, satellites, space probes, computers, all designed to coax more and more new observations out of nature, from quasars trillions of light-years away to particles a billionth of a millimeter in diameter to the discovery that electromagnetic rays are nothing but radiant mass and mass is frozen electromagnetic radiation: never before had man observed nature so closely that she stood virtually naked before him, yes, denuded of all her secrets, exploited, her resources squandered, which was why it occasionally seemed to him, D., that nature, for her part, was observing man and becoming aggressive, for what was the pollution of air, earth, and water, what were the dying forests, but a strike, a deliberate refusal to neutralize the poisons, while the new viruses, earthquakes, droughts, floods, hurricanes, volcanic eruptions, et cetera, were precisely aimed defensive measures of observed nature against her observer, much the way D.'s mirror telescope and the rocks that were thrown at his house were measures taken against being observed, or, for that matter, von Lambert's

manner of observing his wife and her manner of
observing him, in each case a process of objectifi-
cation pursued to a degree that could only be unbearable to the other, the doctor turning the wife
into an object of psychoanalytic scrutiny and she
turning him into an object of hate until, struck by
the sudden insight that she, the observer, was
being observed by the observed, she spontaneously
threw her red fur coat over her denim suit and
fled the vicious circle of mutual observation, and
met with her death, but, he added, after suddenly bursting into laughter and becoming serious
again, what he was constructing here was of course
only one of two possibilities, the other one being
the precise opposite of what he had described, for
a logical conclusion always depends on the initial
situation: if, in his house in the mountains, he
was being observed less and less, so rarely that,
when he pointed his mirror telescope at people
who he presumed were observing him from the
cliff, they turned out to be observing not him but
something else through their field glasses, chamois
or mountain climbers or whatnot, this state of not
being observed would begin to torment him after
a while, much more than the knowledge of being
observed had bothered him earlier, so that he would
virtually yearn for those rocks to be thrown at his

house, because not being watched would make him feel not worth noticing, not being worth noticing would make him feel disrespected, being disrespected would make him feel insignificant, being insignificant would make him feel meaningless, and, he imagined, the end result might be a hopeless depression, in fact he might even give up his unsuccessful academic career as meaningless, and would have to conclude that other people suffered as much from not being observed as he did, that they, too, felt meaningless unless they were being observed, and that this was the reason why they all observed and took snapshots and movies of each other, for fear of experiencing the meaninglessness of their existence in the face of a dispersing universe with billions of Milky Ways like our own, settled with countless of life-bearing but hopelessly remote and therefore isolated planets like our own, a cosmos filled with incessant pulsations of exploding and collapsing suns, leaving no one, except man himself, to pay any attention to man and thereby lend him meaning, for a personal god was no longer possible in the face of such a monstrosity as this universe, a god as world regent and father who keeps an eye on everyone, who counts the hairs on every head, this god was dead because he had become inconceivable, an axiom of faith without any roots in human understanding, only an impersonal god was still conceivable as an abstract principle, as a philosophical-literary construct with which to magically smuggle some kind of meaning into the monstrous whole, vague and vaporous, feeling is all, the name nothing but sound and fury, nebulous glow of heaven locked in the porcelain stove of the heart, but the intellect too, he said, was incapable of coming up with a persuasive illusion of meaning outside of man, for everything that could be thought or done, logic, metaphysics, mathematics, natural law, art, music, poetry, was given its meaning by man, and without man, it sank back into the realm of the unimagined and unconceived and hence into meaninglessness, and a great deal of what was happening today became understandable if one pursued this line of reasoning, man was staggering along in the mad hope of somehow finding someone to be observed by somewhere, by conducting an arms race, for instance, for of course the powers engaged in an arms race were forced to observe one another, which was why they basically hoped to be able to keep up the arms race forever, so that they would have to observe one another forever, since without an arms race, the contending powers would sink into insignificance, but if by some mishap the arms race should set off the nuclear fireworks, which it had been quite capable of accomplishing for some time, it would represent nothing more than a meaningless manifestation of the fact that the earth had once been inhabited, a fireworks without anyone to observe it, unless it were some kind of humanity or similar life-form somewhere near Sirius or elsewhere, without any chance of communicating to the one who so badly desired to be observed (since he would no longer exist) that, in fact, he *had* been observed, and even the religious and political fundamentalism that was breaking out or persisting wherever one looked was an indication that many, indeed most, people could not stand themselves if they were not observed by someone, and would flee either into the fantasy of a personal god or into an equally metaphysically conceived political party that (or who) would observe them, a condition from which they in turn would derive the right to observe whether the world was heeding the laws of the all-observing god or party—except for the terrorists, their case was a bit more complex, their goal being not an observed but an unobserved child's paradise, but because they experienced the world in which they lived as a prison where they were not only unjustly locked up but were left unattended and unobserved in one of the dungeons, they desperately sought to force themselves on the attention of their guards and thus step out of their unobserved condition into the limelight of public notice, which, however, they could achieve only by, paradoxically, drawing back into unobserved obscurity again and again, from the dungeon into the dungeon, unable, ever, to come out and be free, in short, humanity was about to return to its swaddling clothes, fundamentalists, idealists, moralists, and political Christers were doing their utmost to saddle unobserved humanity with the blessings of being observed, and therefore with meaning, for man, in the final analysis, was a pedant who couldn't get by without meaning and was therefore willing to put up with anything except the freedom to not give a damn about meaning—like Tina von Lambert: she, too, had dreamed of drawing upon herself the observing eyes of the world, so perhaps one could read her doubly underlined sentence "I am being observed" as a statement of certainty about the victorious outcome of her enterprise, but, if one accepted this possibility, it would be just the beginning of the actual tragedy, in that her husband did not recognize her flight as an attempt to make others observe her, but, interpreting it as an escape from being observed, failed to undertake an investigation, thus scotching her plans from the outset, and she, upon finding that her disappearance remained unobserved, which is to say, ignored, may have felt impelled to seek out more and more audacious adventures, until, by her death, she achieved the desired end, her picture in all the papers and all the world observing her and giving her the recognition and meaning for which she had yearned.

||| 6 ||| F., who had listened attentively to the logician and had ordered a Campari, said she supposed D. wondered why she had accepted von Lambert's assignment, that the difference between observing and being observed was an entertaining logical game, but not as interesting to her as what he had said earlier about man's not ever being identical with himself because he was always an other, thrown into time, if she had properly understood D., which, however, would mean that there was no self, or rather, only a countless chain of selves emerging from the future, flashing into the present, and sinking back into the past, so that what one commonly called one's self was merely a

collective term for all the selves gathered up in the past, a great heap of selves perpetually growing under the constant rain of selves drifting down through the present from the future, an accumulation of shreds of experience and memory, comparable to a mound of leaves that grows higher and higher under a steady drift of other falling leaves, while the ones at the bottom have long turned to humus, a process that seemed to imply a fiction of selfhood in which every person made up his own self, imagining himself playing a role for better or worse, which would make the possession of character mainly a matter of putting on a good act, and the more unconscious and unintentional the performance, the more genuine its effect, all of which would go a long way toward explaining why it was so hard to make a portrait of an actor, they tended to perform their own character a little too obviously, their intentional actorishness appeared false, looking back on her career and the people she had portrayed gave her the feeling of having made movies of cheap hams, for the most part, especially the politicians, only a few of whom had been capable of putting on a major performance of themselves, which was why she had decided to give up making film portraits, but while reading Tina von Lambert's diary last night, over and over, and trying to imagine this young woman striding off into the desert in a red fur coat, walking in an ocean of sand and stone, she, F., had realized that she would have to follow that woman's trail with her crew and go to the Al-Hakim ruin, come what may, because there in the desert, she sensed, was a reality she would have to meet, just like Tina, and if, for Tina, that reality had been death, it remained to be seen what it would be for her, and then, draining her glass of Campari, she asked D. whether he thought it was crazy of her to accept this assignment, to which D. replied that she should go to the desert because she was looking for a new role, her old role had been that of an observer of roles, and now she wanted to attempt the opposite, not portraiture, which presupposed a subject, but reconstruction, raking together scattered leaves to build up the subject of her portrait, never being sure, all the while, whether the leaves she was heaping up actually belonged together, or whether, in fact, she wasn't ultimately making a self-portrait, in short, a crazy enterprise, but, on the other hand, so crazy that it wasn't crazy, and he wished her well.

||| 7 ||| If the morning had already been humid, almost like summer, at the moment when she stepped up to her car there was a thunderclap, and she rolled up the top of her convertible just in time to avoid a downpour, through which she drove past the center of town to the old market and parked, ignoring a NO STOPPING sign, she had not been mistaken, the address hastily scribbled on one page of the journal was that of a studio belonging to an artist who had recently died, he had moved away from the city many years ago, no doubt someone else was using it, if it was still in existence at all, for it had fallen into such lamentable disrepair that she was convinced it

27

would have been demolished by now, but because the address must have something to do with Tina von Lambert (otherwise it could not have appeared in the journal), she ran the short distance between her car and the door of the building through the pouring rain, and although the door was not locked, she was drenched by the time she had entered the hallway, which had not changed, the hard rain was splashing against the cobblestones of the court-yard, nothing had changed there either, there was the shed that had served as the artist's studio, everything the same, and surprisingly, even the door was open, but the stairs led up into darkness, she searched in vain for a light switch, climbed the stairs, holding her hands out in front of her, reached another door and was in the studio, and there, too, in the dim silvery light shining in through the two rainwashed windows, amazingly, nothing had changed, the long, narrow room was still full of the painter's works, large-scale portraits, the most adventurous denizens of the industrial suburb were standing all about, the con men, the winos, the professionally unemployed, bagmen, street preachers, pimps, smugglers, and other artists of life, most of them under the ground now, no doubt less ceremoniously interred than the painter, whose funeral she remembered, conceivably some weeping prostitutes had come, or some drinking buddies who poured beer on the grave, assuming there had been a funeral at all and not a cremation, portraits she had presumed, in fact seen, in museums, and at the feet of these figures who were no longer present except on canvas stood smaller pictures, representing a streetcar, toilets, pans, wrecked cars, bicycles, umbrellas, traffic policemen, Cinzano bottles, there was nothing the painter had not depicted, the disorder was tremendous, in front of a huge, half-torn leather armchair stood a box, on top of it slices of air-dried beef on a tray, Chianti bottles on the floor and a water glass half filled with wine, newspapers, eggshells, paint spots everywhere, as if the artist were still alive, brushes, palettes, bottles of turpentine and petroleum, the only thing missing was a scaffold, the rain slapped against the two windows on the long wall to her left, and in order to see better, F. removed a secretary of state and a bank director (who for the past two years had been leading a somewhat diminished existence in jail) to let in some light from a third window in the back, and found herself standing before a painting of a woman in a red fur coat, which F. at first took for a portrait of Tina von Lambert, but which turned out not to be Tina after all, it could just as well be a portrait of a woman who looked like Tina, and then, with a shock, it seemed to her that this woman standing before her defiantly with wide-open eyes was herself, and at the precise moment when this thought shot through her, she heard steps behind her and turned around, but too late, the door had slammed shut, and when she returned to the studio with her crew in the late afternoon, the portrait had disappeared, and a film crew was shooting the studio, a reconstruction, according to the peculiarly giddy director, the idea was to give an impression, before the opening of the retrospective exhibition at the museum, of how the studio had looked when the artist was using it, no one had used it since then, they searched through the catalog, the portrait was not listed, and besides, it was simply not possible that the studio would have been left unlocked.

||| 8 ||| Still confused by this experience, which seemed to her like a sign that she was searching in the wrong direction, she nearly canceled her flight, but checked the impulse, the preparations took their course, already they were flying over Spain, beneath them the Guadalquivir, the Atlantic came into view, and when they landed in C., she began to look forward to the trip inland, the trees would probably still be green, and she remembered a road lined with date palms that she had seen on a previous trip several years ago, cars coming toward her on the way back from the snow-covered Atlas mountains with skis on their roofs; however, right after landing, still on the runway, she and

her crew were picked up by the police and taken with all their equipment and without having to pass through customs to a military transport plane and flown to the country's interior, to be driven at breakneck speed from the airport at M. to the city, past throngs of tourists who craned their necks as she passed, escorted by four policemen on motor-cycles and accompanied by a TV crew in two cars with incessantly running cameras, one car in front of her, one behind, all the way to the police ministry, where F. and her crew were filmed while filming the police chief as he leaned against his desk in his white uniform, incredibly fat, remi-niscent of Göring, voicing his pleasure at having the opportunity, despite his government's mis-givings, to allow F. and her crew to inspect and film the site of the gruesome misdeed, and his particular pleasure at learning that, in her effort to reconstruct the crime, F. would be documenting the impeccable work of his police force, who were equipped with the most modern weapons and not only met but exceeded international standards, a shameless proposal that reinforced the suspicion F. had been harboring ever since her experience in the artist's studio, that she was on the wrong trail, for already her enterprise, scarcely begun, had been rendered meaningless by this fat man who was constantly wiping the sweat off his forehead with a silk handkerchief and to whom all she represented was a source of publicity for himself and his police, but, having once entered the trap, she could see no immediate way to escape it, for it was not just the police who were holding her and her crew captive by leading them to a jeep whose turbaned driver (all the other policemen wore white helmets) motioned F. to sit down next to him while the cameraman and the sound technician sat down behind her and the assistant carrying the equipment had to board a second jeep, driven by a black man—the TV crew, too, was following them as they approached the desert, to the annoyance of F., who would have preferred to gather information first but had no way of explaining herself, because, whether by design or by negligence, no interpreter was present and the policemen accompanying her or rather bossing her around did not have the command of French one might have expected in this country, and also because the TV crew was racing out of earshot into the stone desert, off to the side of F.'s jeep, the caravan falling into such disarray that the other cars, including the jeep with the assistant and the equipment, seemed to be moving apart in the boiling distance, each according to its driver's whim, even the four motorcycle cops who were supposed to form her escort veered from her jeep and zoomed off, chasing each other, chugged back in her direction, then leaned away again in wide arcs, while the TV crew shot straight toward the horizon and presently vanished out of sight, but as if to make up for that, her driver, stammering some incomprehensible sounds, set off in pursuit of a jackal, curving after it, the jackal running, running, throwing feints, changing direction abruptly, always tailed by the jeep, which seemed on the verge of capsizing several times, while F. and the cameraman and the sound technicians clung to their seats, then the motorcyclists came roaring by, yelling and making signs that were undecipherable to them, until suddenly they had left the stone desert and were tearing along a macadam road through vast stretches of sand, with no other vehicle in sight, even the four motorcyclists had disappeared, somehow, unaccountably, the driver who had been unable to run down the jackal had managed to find this road, even though it was partially covered over with sand, and now the desert on either side looked to F. like an ocean plowed up by the jeeps as if by a ship's prow, waves of sand towering up on either side as the shadows grew longer, when all of a sudden the Al-Hakim ruin rose up before them from a depression into which they flew un-expectedly, straight toward the monument which loomed up before her from the swarming cluster of policemen and television people who had already gathered in front of it, black, obscuring the sun, the enigmatic witness of an unimaginably ancient time, discovered around the turn of the century as a huge flat stone square, polished smooth as a mirror by the sand, which turned out to be the top surface of a cube and, as the excavations continued, acquired ever more impressive dimensions, but when plans were made to uncover the whole of it, some saints of a Shiʾite sect, emaciated and covered with rags, had squatted down by one of the sides of the cube, wrapped in black cloaks, waiting for the mad caliph Al-Hakim, who, according to their belief, lurked inside the cube and was about to burst forth any month, any day, any minute, any second, to assume dominion over the world, they huddled like great black birds, no one dared chase them away, the archaeologists dug up the other three sides of the cube, reaching deeper and deeper, while the black Sufis, as they were called, sat far above them, always motionless, even when the wind covered them with sand, visited only once a week by a gigantic Negro who came riding on a donkey to shove a spoonful of cereal into their

35

mouths and splash water over their heads, and of whom it was said that he was still a slave, and when F. approached them—because a young police officer, suddenly in full command of the French language, had explained to her that Tina's body had been found among these "saints," as he respectfully called them, and that someone must have dropped her there, though it was impossible to obtain any information from them, since they had taken a vow of silence until the return of their "Mahdi"—when she came closer and gazed for a long time at the long rows of silent, crouching, mummylike men who seemed to have become one with the black squares of the cube, a fungus emerging from one of its flanks, long, white, stringy, sand-encrusted beards, the eyes invisible in their black sockets, densely covered with crawling masses of flies, hands clasped like claws with long fingernails penetrating the palms, and then, cautiously, touched one of them to see if perhaps she might get some information after all, he keeled over, it was a corpse, so was the one next to him, the cameras behind her whirred, the third man gave the impression of still being alive, but she gave up, only her cameraman strode down the length of the row with the camera pressed to his eye, and when she reported the incident to the police officer,

who had stayed by his car, he replied that the
jackals would take care of the rest, Tina's body,
too, he said, had been found torn and partially
eaten, and at that moment dusk set in, the sun
must have set behind the depression, and it seemed
to F. that night was attacking her like a merciful
enemy who kills quickly.

‖ 9 ‖ The next day, before F. could book a return flight, the cameraman informed her that the exposed footage had disappeared, someone had switched the rolls of film, the TV people had insisted it *was* his footage, the cameraman had then demanded furiously, and was promised, that the rolls would be developed by the evening, too late to catch a plane, and once again they were being abducted by the police, and this in a manner that made it seem wiser to pretend compliance: after being led into the subterranean prison compound at the police ministry, they were introduced to prisoners whom F. was permitted to question and film, each man was relieved of his handcuffs the moment he entered the room, but after he had sat down on the stool he was offered, a policeman would press a submachine gun into the back of his neck, they were badly shaved, all of them, with missing teeth, greedily reaching for the cigarettes F. offered them, and when asked if they had seen the woman in this picture, they would briefly glance at the snapshot of Tina and nod, and when F. asked them where, they would quietly answer, "In the ghetto," all of them wearing dirty white linen pants and jackets, no shirts, as if in uniform and all of them with the same answer: in the ghetto, in the ghetto, in the ghetto, and each one told her how someone had tried to hire him to kill the woman in the picture, she was the wife of a man who had defended the Arab resistance movement and hadn't called it a terrorist organization, or something like that, he hadn't been able to figure out why the woman was supposed to die for that, he had refused the offer, it hadn't been enough money, there were fixed tariffs for this kind of thing, a question of honor, the man who had made the offer was short and fat, an American, probably, or—that was all he knew, he had only seen the woman once, in the fat man's company, in the ghetto, as he'd already explained, all the others gave similar statements, mechanically, greedily smoking their cigarettes, only one of them grinned when he saw the picture, blew smoke into F.'s face, he was small, almost dwarfish, with a big wrinkled face, spoke English more or less the way Scandinavians speak English, said he had never seen this woman, nobody had seen this woman, whereupon the policeman pulled him up to his feet and struck him in the back with his sub-machine gun, but an officer stepped in quickly, barked at the policeman, suddenly other policemen were in the room, the man with the big wrinkled face was led out, a new prisoner was shoved in from outside, sat down in the glare of the arc light, the clapper again, the whirring of the camera, he reached for a cigarette with quivering hands, looked at the picture, told the same story as the others, with insignificant variations, mumbling at times, like the others, because he, like the others, had almost no teeth, then the next man, and then the last, whereupon they left the bare concrete room where they had questioned the men, containing just a wobbly table, an arc light, and some chairs, marched through the subterranean prison world, past iron bars behind which something whitish cowered or lay on the floor, and ascended by elevator to the investigating magistrate's modern and comfortably furnished office, where the magistrate, a gentle, pretty-faced lawyer with rimless glasses that didn't suit him, regaled F. and her crew with every conceivable delicacy, even caviar and vodka (they were sitting on comfortable armchairs around a glass-topped table), while he, the investigating magistrate, dedicated himself assiduously to an Alsatian white wine that a French colleague had sent him, waved off the cameraman, who was already raising his camera, and explained at great length that he was a believing Moslem, in many respects even a fundamentalist, Khomeini has his undeniably positive, even magnificent aspects, but the process leading to a synthesis of the Koran's philosophy of law and European jurisprudence could simply no longer be stopped in this country, it was comparable with the integration of Aristotle into medieval Moslem theology, and finally, after a tiresome, rambling detour by way of the history of the Spanish Umayyads, he returned as if by accident to the case of Tina von Lambert, expressed his regret, his sympathetic understanding of the emotions this case had elicited in Europe, a culture that tended to the tragic view of life, while Islam inclined to fatalism, and produced some photographs of the body, and said, "Oh, well, the jackals," adding that the body had been taken to the Al-Hakim monument after the

killing, which, with all due respect, suggested a
Christian, or—well, you know—perpetrator, no
Moslem would have dared throw the corpse among
the saints, there was general indignation about
that, whereupon he showed them the medical
examiner's report, rape, death by strangulation,
apparently without a struggle, the men presented
to F. downstairs had been foreign agents, and as
for who might have been interested in killing her,
well, there was no need to get too specific, von
Lambert's refusal, at the international antiterrorist
congress, to refer to Arab freedom fighters as terrorists, a certain secret service had felt it necessary to
set an example, one of the agents was the probable
perpetrator, the country was full of spies, including,
naturally, Soviet spies, Czechs, East Germans especially, but mainly American, French, English,
West German, Italian spies, why count them all,
in short, adventurers from all over the world, and
that certain secret service, F. would know who he
was talking about, were by far the most crafty of
all, they hired other agents, that was their perfi-
dious specialty, the killing of Tina von Lambert
was, on the one hand, an act of revenge, and on the
other it was intended to disrupt the good trade
relations between his country and the European
Common Market, especially the export of goods

and products that were the principal source of revenue for—you know—and then, after the investigating magistrate had taken a call, he silently stared at F. and her crew, opened the door, motioned for them to follow, led them through corridors, down a flight of stairs, along further corridors, narrower than the others, until they reached a wall with a number of peepholes through which one could look out upon a bare courtyard that was evidently enclosed by the building, but all they saw were smooth, windowless walls, which made the courtyard look like a shaft, or pit, into which the dwarfish Scandinavian was now led past a row of policemen with white helmets and white gloves and submachine guns slung over their shoulders, he was handcuffed, behind him was a police captain with a drawn sword, the Scandinavian stopped in front of the concrete wall facing the row of policemen, the officer walked back to his men and positioned himself next to the row, held the sword vertically in front of his face, just like a scene in an operetta, and as if to emphasize that, the rotund police chief came in, waddling laboriously, sweating, until he had reached the dwarfish, grinning man by the wall, stuck a cigarette in his mouth, lit it, and slowly waddled out of view, the camera whirred, somehow the cameraman had found a way to record what was happening down below, the dwarfish man smoked, the policemen stood aiming their submachine guns at him (there was something attached to the muzzles, silencers probably), waiting, the officer lowered his sword again, the policemen were growing restless, the officer abruptly raised his sword back to a vertical position, the policemen took aim once again, a dull thud followed, and as the policemen lowered their guns, the dwarfish man reached for the cigarette with his manacled hands, dropped it, extinguished it with his foot, collapsed, and lay on the ground, motionless, blood flowing out of every part of his body toward the center of the courtyard, where there was a drain, and the investigating magistrate, stepping away from his peephole, said the Scandinavian had confessed, he was the killer, regrettably the police chief was given to rash and precipitate actions, however, the general indignation in the country—well—, and back they went, along the narrow passageway, through the iron gate, down corridors, but different ones this time, up stairs and down stairs, then a projection room, the police chief was there already, filling his armchair, gracious, animated by the execution, perfumed rivulets of sweat on his face, smoking ciga-

rettes like the one he had offered the dwarfish man,
in whose confession neither F. nor her crew believed, nor, apparently, the investigating magistrate,
who, muttering another "Oh, well," discreetly with-
drew, on the screen now the Al-Hakim ruin, the
cars, the television crews, the policemen, the four
motorcyclists, the arrival of F. with her crew, the
cameraman instructing the foolishly smiling assistant, the sound technician fussing with his instruments, intermittently the desert, a policeman on a
camel, the jeep, the turbaned driver at the wheel,
finally F. staring at something, but no indication of
what it was: the figures crouching at the foot of the
ruin, those manlike creatures covered with flies,
half submerged in sand, sand sweeping across their
black cloaks, no picture of these, just more policemen, then their training, policemen in classrooms,
in athletic contests, in dormitories, brushing their
teeth, taking showers en masse, the whole thing
applauded by the white-clad Göring, this film, he
declared, was magnificent, yes, he could only con-
gratulate her, and upon F.'s protest that this wasn't
her film at all, he said, "Really?" and immediately
supplied the answer: the material must have been
useless, it was really no wonder in the desert sun,
but the crime was solved now, the perpetrator had

been executed, he wished her a pleasant trip home, whereupon he stood up, graciously took his leave, "Farewell, my child," which F. found particularly annoying, and walked out of the room.

||| **10** ||| Outside the building, the policeman
with the turban was waiting for her at the wheel
of his jeep with a mocking smile, while behind
him, tourists jammed the broad esplanade between the police ministry and the great mosque,
beleaguered by children who pried open the
foreigners' hands, hoping to find some money,
attacked by the barking sounds of a sermon trans-
mitted by loudspeakers from inside the mosque,
and by the tooting and honking of taxis and
tour buses seeking a path through a multiracial
thicket of travelers all busily photographing and
filming each other and forming an unreal contrast
to the secret life inside the compound of the police

47

ministry, like two interlocking realities, one of them cruel and demonic, the other as banal as tourism itself, and when the turbaned policeman addressed F. in French, which he hadn't been able to speak before, it was too much for her: she left her crew, she wanted to be alone, she felt guilty of the little Scandinavian's death, he had only been executed in order to put an end to her investigation, she kept seeing the wrinkled face, the cigarette between his thin lips, then the flies crawling over the skulls of the black-robed men by the Al-Hakim ruin, and it seemed to her that at the moment when she set foot in this country, she had walked into a waking nightmare, and also that, for the first time in her life, she had failed, for if she tried to carry out her assignment, she would be endangering not only her own life but that of her crew, the police chief was dangerous, he would hold back at nothing, some secret was hidden behind Tina von Lambert's death, the investigating magistrate's preachments were all too transparent, a clumsy attempt to hide something, cover it up, but what was it, she didn't know, and then she reproached herself for allowing someone to leave the studio while she was looking at the portrait of the woman in the red fur coat, a face which, at least now, in memory, seemed to resemble her own

more and more, was it a man or a woman who had
been hiding in the studio, had the director kept
something from her, the bed she had discovered
behind the curtain, who had used it, she had
failed to look into this and now she was furious at
herself for being so inefficient, and, jostled by
tourists, she arrived in the old city and suddenly
found it difficult to breathe, an overpowering
smell enveloped her, not a particular smell but
the combined odors of every kind of herb mixed
with the smell of blood and feces, of coffee, honey,
and sweat, she moved through dark, cavernous
streets that were constantly lighting up, since there
was always someone in the crowd taking a picture,
past stacks of copper kettles and bowls, pots, rugs,
jewelry, radios, television sets, suitcases, meat and
fish stands, mountains of vegetables and fruit,
always wrapped in that penetrating cloud of odors
and stenches, until she suddenly brushed against
something furry, and stopped, people squeezing
past her, pressing against her, local people, no more
tourists, she realized with some bewilderment,
above her, suspended from wire hangers, cheap
gaudy skirts of every color, all the more grotesque
since no one wore such skirts, and what she had
brushed against was a red fur coat that she immediately knew was Tina von Lambert's coat, it

must have attracted her magically, so it seemed to her, which was why she almost compulsively entered the store in front of which the clothes were hung, a cavelike place, it took a while before her eyes got used to the dark and she distinguished an old man, whom she addressed but who didn't react, whereupon she seized him by the hand and forced him to follow her outside, beneath his gaudy skirts, disregarding the children who had gathered around and stood staring, wide-eyed, at F., who had torn the fur coat from its hanger and, determined to buy it no matter what the price, realized only then that she was dealing with a blind man whose only piece of clothing was a long dirty garment that had once been white, with a large encrusted spot of blood on the breast, half covered by a gray beard, his face, his eyes, whitish-yellow, without pupils, were immobile, he seemed deaf as well, she took his hand, stroked the fur with it, he didn't answer, the children stood there, the local people stopped, others joined them, wondering what was causing the congestion, the old man still didn't say anything, F. reached into her bag, which she always wore slung over her denim suit, containing, carefree as she was, her passport, her jewelry, her makeup, and her money, pressed some bills into the blind man's hand, put on the coat and walked off through the crowd, accompanied by a few children who jabbered incomprehensible words at her, and then, without any idea of how she had found her way out of the old city or where she was, she found a taxi that brought her to her hotel, where her crew was lounging in the lobby, staring at her as she stood before them in her red fur coat, asked the sound technician for a cigarette and explained that the red fur coat she had found in the center of town had been worn by Tina von Lambert when she went to the desert, and that, absurd as it seemed, she was not going to leave until she had found out the truth about Tina von Lambert's death.

‖ **11** ‖ Does this make sense, asked the sound technician, the assistant grinned uneasily, and the cameraman stood up and said he wasn't going to put up with this nonsense, the minute F. had left them, some cops had come to confiscate the material they had shot in the ministry, and when they arrived at the hotel, the clerk had told them he'd already booked a return flight and arranged for a taxi at the crack of dawn, as far as he was concerned he was fed up with this whole damn country, the men they'd questioned had been tortured, that was why they had no teeth, and the shooting of the dwarf, he'd puked in his room for an hour, it was nuts to stick one's nose in this country's politics, all his fears had been confirmed, this wasn't the place to conduct any sort of research deserving the name, it wasn't just impossible, it was potentially lethal, which wouldn't even matter if he could see the slightest chance of success, and then, throwing himself back in the armchair, he added that the whole project was so vague, frankly so confused, that he could only advise F. to give it up, fine, she'd found a red fur coat, but how could she be sure it was von Lambert's coat, to which F. replied with irritation that she had never given up anything, and when the sound technician, who loved nothing more than peace, suggested it might be better if she left with them because some facts were by nature undiscoverable, she went up to her room without saying a word, did not cross the threshold, however, for there in the armchair beneath the lamp sat the gentle, pretty-faced man with rimless glasses, the investigating magistrate, who returned F.'s long, wordless gaze, and then, with a movement of his hand, invited her to sit down on the second armchair, which she did, mechanically, because it seemed to her as if behind those soft, sentimental features she could discern something hard and determined that had been previously hidden, his language, too, as he began to talk, congratulating her for her discovery of Tina von Lambert's coat, was no longer circumlocutious, but hard, accurate, and often sarcastic, like that of a man who enjoys hoodwinking an opponent, so that all she could do was wordlessly nod when he informed her that he had come to thank her for the material she had filmed, the black saints and the execution of the Dane were marvelously suited to his purposes, and when she asked what his purposes were, he calmly replied that, incidentally, he had taken the liberty of having a bottle of Chablis added to the usual fruit juices, lemonades, and mineral waters in the refrigerator, and that next to the refrigerator was a bottle of whiskey, and when she said she preferred whiskey, he said he had thought so, there were nuts, too, stood up, opened the re-frigerator, returned with two glasses of whiskey, ice, and nuts, introduced himself as the head of the secret service, well informed about her habits, and he hoped she would forgive all the babbling in the ministry, the police chief had bugged every conceivable nook and cranny, he, too, incidentally, could hear anything the police chief listened to, any time he wished, and then, with a few words, he told her that the police chief was planning a coup, that he wanted to change the country's foreign policy, blame a foreign secret service for the murder of Tina, hence the shooting of the Dane, but the police chief had no idea that the execution was on film, nor did he know he was being watched by the head of the secret service, he didn't even know who the head of the secret service was, all the police chief wanted was to look like a strong man who could use the police as his private army, so that, once he took over, his power would look secure from the start, but he, the head of the secret service, intended to expose the chief of police, to show how he had corrupted the police and how weak his power really was, how unstable and already crumbling, but his main concern, he said, was to use the case of Tina von Lambert to prove the police chief's incompetence, which was why he had done everything possible to make F.'s investigation possible, with a new crew, of course, he would supply her with a new one, the police chief must be kept in the dark, her old crew would leave, he, the head of the secret service, had made all the arrangements, instructed the necessary people, the hotel personnel were acting on his instructions, a friend of his would assume her role, come in, please, at which point the door opened and a young woman entered, dressed in the same denim suit F. was wearing, with a red fur coat slung over her shoulder, cut exactly like

Tina von Lambert's, a detail that prompted F. to ask whether she should take his request as an order, to which he replied that it was she who had accepted von Lambert's assignment, and that he, the head of the secret service, regarded it as his duty to assist her in carrying out that assignment, and then he added that he would have F. put up somewhere else, she had nothing to fear, from now on she was under his protection, but it would be good if she would inform her crew, without, however, telling them more than was strictly necessary, for her own sake, whereupon he said good-bye and led the young woman out of the room, who resembled F. only to the extent that, from a distance, they could conceivably be mistaken for one another.

||| 12 ||| The cameraman was already in bed when F. called him, he went to her room in his pajamas, found her packing her bags, listened silently to her report, in which she left out nothing, not even the advice of the head of the secret service that she keep all but the most necessary details to herself, and not until she had finished did he pour himself a whiskey, which he then forgot to drink, he reflected on what he had heard and finally said that F. had fallen into a trap, it wasn't by accident that Tina von Lambert's red fur coat had ended up in a blind vendor's shop in the old city, that red fur coat had been the bait, there weren't many coats like that, maybe just one, and

57

the fact that this other woman was wearing the same kind of coat proved they were planning something very carefully, they'd expected F. would go to the old city, a red fur coat hanging among cheap skirts would attract anyone's attention, and tailoring a second coat for her double wasn't something you could do in a hurry, that the head of the secret service wanted to˙ put the police chief out of commission made sense, but why should he need F. to do that, why go to such lengths, something else was afoot here, Tina von Lambert hadn't come to this country just out of a whim, there must have been a reason, a reason that had something to do with her death, he had read von Lambert's book on terrorism, there were two pages devoted to the Arab resistance movement, von Lambert refused to call them terrorists, which didn't preclude, and he had emphasized this, that nonterrorists were also capable of atrocities, Auschwitz, for instance, was not the work of terrorists but of state employees, in short it was out of the question that Tina von Lambert had been murdered on account of her husband's book, the head of the secret service was keeping the truth hidden from her just like everyone else, she had walked right into his open knife and there was no turning back now, but she had been careless in telling him,

58

the cameraman, everything, he'd be very surprised if the head of the secret service let her crew leave the country, she should wish him good luck, he'd wish her the same, and he embraced her and left without touching his whiskey, something he had never done before, and F. suddenly had the feeling she would never see him again, her thoughts turned back to the artist's studio, and now she was sure the footsteps behind her had been a woman's, she furiously downed the glass of whiskey and went on packing, shut the suitcase, put on the red fur coat over her denim suit, left the room, and was shown the way through the back door of the hotel by an unlikely looking bellboy, who carried her suitcase and led her to a jeep, where two men in burnouses were waiting for her and drove her out of the city, first by a main road, then on a dusty road past fields of snow and rocky banks, barely visible in the moonless night, down steep ravines and up again, deeper into the mountains toward something like walls shimmering far away in the first light of dawn, which, when they stopped and got out of the car, turned out to be a weathered three-story house with a sign reading GRAND HÔTEL MARÉCHAL LYAUTEY above the front door, which was slamming open and shut in the icy wind, and there one of the men—since no one

came to the dimly lit lobby in response to his call
—assigned her to a room on the second floor, simply
by opening a door, shoving her inside, and dumping
the suitcase on the wooden floor, after which she,
surprised by the rude treatment, heard him stomp-
ing downstairs and then taking off in the jeep,
apparently back to M., looked around her room,
irritated, a bulb hanging from the ceiling, the
shower out of order, shreds of wallpaper hanging
from the walls, a rickety chair and an army cot
the only pieces of furniture, but the bed was
freshly made, and over and over, the front door
slammed open and shut, even after falling asleep
she could hear the door.

||| **13** ||| When she awoke, perhaps because the door had stopped slamming, it was already noon, and through the window, which was so dirty the daylight barely shimmered through, she looked out on a landscape riddled with ravines and covered with shrubs, behind it a steep, abruptly jutting mountain ridge, its top hid in a cloud that looked caught on the ice-covered cliffs and crags and appeared to be boiling in the sunlight, a gloomy sight that made her wonder, as she walked down the wooden staircase (wrapped in the red fur coat, for it was bitterly cold), what this "hotel" had ever been built for, and what was its purpose now, no one was downstairs, she called, the lobby

6 1

was empty, nothing more than a shabby room actually, no one in the kitchen either, until the sound of slippered feet came from a neighboring room and an old woman entered and stopped in the door, staring at F. as if shocked, until she finally pressed out the words, in French, "Her coat, her coat," pointing at the red fur coat with a quivering hand, "her coat," babbling these words over and over, and obviously so bewildered that when F. approached her she retreated into the room next door, which had apparently once served as a dining room, and positioned herself behind the dinner table and some old chairs, waiting anxiously for F., who, however, not wishing to frighten the old woman any further, stayed in the dreary lobby (its only decoration was a large, framed, yellowing portrait of a French general, apparently Marshal Lyautey) and asked in French if she could have some breakfast, which the old woman affirmed with several intense nods, stepping up to F., taking her by the hand and pulling her to a terrace where, against the wall of the house under a torn awning that had once been orange, there stood a wooden table, already set, breakfast was ready as well, for the old woman served it immediately after F. had sat down, and if all she had seen from her room was a welter of bushes, rocks, and ravines with the boiling mountain ridge in the background, now F. had a view of a gentle, still verdant hill and several lower hills abutting against it and breaking against each other like waves and descending far down to a shimmering whitish-yellow color, the desert, and it seemed to her that, at the outermost edge of the eye's reach, she could half discern, half surmise something black, the Al-Hakim ruin, the wind was chilly, F. was glad to be able to hug the red fur coat around herself, which the old woman glanced at again and again, stroking it, too, shyly, almost tenderly, as she hovered next to F., as if to watch over her as she ate her breakfast, but the moment F. asked her if she had known Tina von Lambert, she started at the sound of the name and seemed confused again, pointing at the coat and stammering, "Tina, Tina, Tina," then asked F. whether she was a friend, and when F. said yes, she began to talk with great excitement, and what F. thought she was able to make out of this stuttering, garbled communication was that Tina had come here in a rented car (the woman repeated the word "alone" several times, and kept stammering something incomprehensible about the rented car), that she had rented a room for three months and driven around the area and all the way down to the desert, even up to the black stone (by which she evidently meant the ruin), until suddenly she didn't come back, but she, the old woman, knew, though what it was that she knew was impossible to understand, no matter how hard F. tried to make out the meaning of the stammered, repetitive, fractured sentences, the old woman suddenly stopped talking, her face frozen with mistrust, staring at the red fur coat, and F., who had finished her breakfast, sensing that the old woman wanted to ask something but did not dare, decided to tell her, not without a certain brutality, that Tina would not come back, that she was dead, to which the old woman at first responded with indifference, as if she had not understood what she had heard, but suddenly she began to grimace, and to giggle to herself, in despair, as F. gradually realized, and, taking the old woman by the shoulder and shaking her, she demanded to be shown the room Tina had rented, whereupon the old woman, still giggling, mumbled something that sounded like "all the way up," and F. walked up the stairs, ignoring the sound of the old woman's sudden sobs, for here on the third floor she had found a room that had possibly been Tina von Lambert's, a better room than the one F. had slept in, comfortably furnished in a style that was out of keeping with the rest of the hotel, surprising to F. as she

64

looked around: a wide bed with an old coverlet of an undefinable color, a fireplace that had evidently never been used, some volumes of Jules Verne on the mantelpiece, above it the portrait of Marshal Lyautey, an antique writing desk, a bathroom with a partly damaged tile wall and rust spots in the tub, torn velvet curtains, and as she stepped out onto the balcony facing the distant desert, she saw something disappearing behind a little stone wall about a hundred meters down the hill in the direction of the desert, she waited, and then it came back, it was the head of a man watching her through binoculars, which reminded her of Tina's doubly underlined sentence, "I am being watched," and when she stepped back into the room, the old woman was standing there with the suitcase, the bathrobe, and F.'s purse, and sheets and pillowcases as well, matter-of-factly, as if this were the expected thing to do, whereupon F. asked with irritation where she could make a call, was directed down the stairs, found the telephone in a dark hallway next to the kitchen, and, following a defiant impulse, decided to call D., the logician, convinced she would not be able to get through, but determined to attempt the impossible nevertheless, lifted the receiver, and found the line dead, no doubt a precaution taken by the head of the

secret service, it was he who had arranged to have
her brought here, where Tina von Lambert had
been, but suddenly she mistrusted the reasons he
had given her, especially because she could not
imagine what could have prompted Tina to drive
around in the desert, as the old woman had told
her, and, sitting on the floor by the open balcony
door, then lying in bed and staring up at the
ceiling, she tried to reconstruct Tina von Lambert's
fate, starting again from the only reliable point of
departure, Tina's journals, and tried to imagine
every possible scenario leading up to the end,
Tina's body torn by jackals in front of the Al-
Hakim ruin, but none of them seemed convincing,
the way she had left the house, "straight away,"
as von Lambert had put it, suggested a flight, but
she had come to this country, not like a fugitive
but as if pursuing a definite goal, like a journalist
tracking down secret information, but Tina wasn't
a journalist, a love affair was conceivable, but there
was no indication of a love affair, she stepped outside the hotel later without having found a solu-
tion, the cloud on top of the mountain had grown,
had begun to push off in her direction, she went
back along the road by which she had come, arrived
at a stony plateau, the road forked, she chose a road
that forked again after half an hour, went back,

waited for a long time in front of her hotel, which stood there, meaningless, solitary, with its door slamming open and shut again, and with the sign above the door, GRAND HÔTEL MARÉCHAL LYAUTEY and above the sign the black rectangle of a window, the only one in the wall, which must once have been white and was now covered with every possible shade of gray blending into all the colors of the spectrum, as if ages ago some giants had vomited it into existence, and it was not only while standing there looking at the hotel and up at the window behind which she had slept, but hours before, actually right after leaving the hotel, that she knew and had known that she was being watched, even though she didn't see anyone watching her, and when the ball-like sun sank behind the faraway desert, so quickly, all of a sudden, as if it were dropping, and dusk descended, leaving only the top layers of the mighty cloud bank lit, like burning sand, and she went back inside, dinner was already served under the portrait of the marshal, lamb in a red sauce, white bread, and red wine, the old woman wasn't there, she ate only a little food, drank some wine, and went up to the room where Tina von Lambert had stayed, stepped out onto the balcony, for it had seemed to her while eating that she had heard distant thunder, the cloud front must have retreated, the wintry stars were burning before and above her, but on the horizon she could see a glaring reflection and a dart of lightning, it was a thunderstorm and yet it wasn't, and suspended over everything was that distant, indefinite grumbling, and again it seemed to her as if, from the darkness that reached up to her from below, she was being watched, and back in the room, already in her bathrobe, which she used for sleeping as well, she shuddered as she stared at the rusty bathtub, when she heard a car approaching the house but passing by without stopping, followed by a second car, which stopped, then the sound of a voice calling, someone must have come into the house, more calls, asking if anyone was there, steps climbing up to the first floor, "Hello, hello," and when F. went down, her red fur coat thrown over her bathrobe, she saw a young man with straw-blond hair about to come up the stairs to where she was, wearing blue corduroy trousers, jogging shoes, and a padded jacket, who gaped at her with wide-open eyes and stammered "Thank God, thank God," and when she asked what there was to thank God for, he raced up the stairs and embraced her and shouted, "That you're alive," and went on to tell her that he'd told the boss and betted that she was still alive and here she was, alive, at which point he leaped down the stairs and down the second flight too, and when F., following him, had reached the hallway, she saw the straw-blond man bringing in suitcases, which led her to believe that he might be the promised cameraman, and when she asked him, he replied, "You guessed it," and brought the camera out of the car, a VW bus, she noticed, looking through the open door, then he made some adjustment on the camera, explaining that he could use this one at night, too, special attachments, and he thought her reports were fantastic, an odd remark that prompted her to ask him if he wouldn't like to introduce himself, at which point he turned red and stammered that his name was Björn Olsen, and they could speak Danish if she wished, which reminded her of the grinning dwarfish man who had stood with his back to the wall, smoking, the way he had collapsed while crushing the cigarette with his foot, and she said she didn't speak Danish, he must be mistaking her for someone else, which almost caused him to drop the camera, and shouting and stamping his foot on the ground, no, no, that couldn't be true, how could she be wearing the same red fur coat, he carried the camera and the suitcases back into the bus, climbed in, and drove off, not back to M. though, but toward the mountains, and when she went back to her room, an explosion suddenly shook the house, but everything was quiet when she stepped back out onto the balcony, the distant flickering and the glaring reflections over the desert were gone, only the stars burned with such icy menace that she went back into the room and pulled the torn velvet curtains shut, and as she did that, her glance fell on the secretary, it was unlocked and empty, and only then did she notice the wastepaper basket next to the desk, and inside it a bunched-up piece of paper, which she unfolded and smoothed out, and on it, in a handwriting that was unfamiliar to her, was a statement in quotation marks, in a Nordic language, incomprehensible to her, but, stubborn as she was, she sat down at the desk and tried to translate the words, some of which, *edderkop*, for instance, or *tomt rum* or *fodfaeste*, gave her some trouble, but by midnight she felt she had solved the riddle: "What should come, what should strange times (*fremtiden*) bring? I do not know, I have no presentiment. When a black widow (*edderkop?*) plunges down from a fixed point to its consequences, it constantly sees an empty space (*tomt rum?*) before it, in which it cannot find a firm foothold (*fodfaeste?*), no matter how it kicks about. Thus is it with me: before me perpetually an empty space (*tomt rum?*), what drives me forward is a consequence that lies behind (*bag*) me. This life is backward (*bagvendt*) and puzzling (*raedsomt?*), intolerable."

|| **14** || When she went downstairs the next morning, wrapped in her red fur coat, determined to walk in the direction of the mountains after breakfast, because she couldn't stop thinking about the explosion after the Dane's departure, and because the quotation, conceivably a coded message, increased her uneasiness, she found the head of the secret service eating breakfast at the wooden table on the terrace, dressed all in white with a black cravat, wearing a pair of heavy-framed shades in place of the rimless glasses, who stood up, invited F. to sit down next to him, poured her a cup of coffee, offered her croissants, which he had brought from the European section of M., ex-

pressed his regrets at having had to lodge her in such poor quarters, and placed in front of her, after she had eaten, a gossip magazine with a picture on the front page of a radiant Tina von Lambert embracing her husband, and a caption beneath it reading "Return from the Dead," the wife of the famous psychiatrist had fallen into a depression and gone into hiding in the studio of a deceased painter, her passport and her red fur coat had been stolen, which had evidently led to her being confused with that woman who was murdered near the Al-Hakim ruin, the riddle now being not only the murderer's identity but also that of the deceased woman, at which point F., her face white with indignation, threw the scandal sheet onto the table, the whole thing was too banal, at the same time she felt so thoroughly humiliated at having allowed herself to be lured into this ridiculous adventure that she would have burst into tears if the iron calm of the head of the secret service next to her hadn't forced her to relax, especially when he explained to her that what was wrong with the story was the theft, Tina had been friends with a Danish journalist, Jytte Sörensen, and had given her the red fur coat and her passport, that was the only way the Danish woman could have entered the country, a piece of information that made F. sit up straight,

and as he poured her another cup of coffee she
asked him how he knew that, and he replied that
he knew because he had interrogated the Danish
woman, she had admitted everything, and when
F. asked why she had been murdered, he breathed
on the lenses of his shades, polished them, and
said this was something he did not know, Jytte
Sörensen had been a very energetic sort of person
who reminded him of F. in more ways than one,
he had not been able to find out why she had
disguised her identity, but since the chief of police
had fallen for it, he had seen no reason to send
her packing with her false passport and her red
fur coat, why should he have, he was sorry she
had come to such a terrible end, had she confided
in him she would still be alive, he presumed F.
had read the crumpled piece of paper in the waste-
basket, it was by Kierkegaard, *Either/Or*, he had
hired a specialist, at first he had thought it must
be a coded message, but now he was convinced it
was a cry for help, he had been able to keep an eye
on this reckless woman until she moved into this
hotel, after that he had lost track of her, he hoped
that tall young man would be luckier than his coun-
trywoman—if that was the right expression—, it
seemed both of them had come on an assignment
from a private Danish television station known for

its sensationalist reportage, and if F., disguised in her red fur coat as someone other than she had first believed, were to go to the mountains or perhaps even to the desert, he would not be able to help her any longer, the crew he had tried to hire had refused to work with him, nor, regrettably, had he been able to permit her crew to leave the country, unfortunately F. had ignored his warning and told them everything, this shabby hotel was the last controllable spot, from here on she would be traveling in no-man's-land, unprotected by international law, but he would be glad to drive her back, whereupon F., after asking him for a cigarette and letting him light it, declared that she would go anyway.

||| **15** ||| When she left the hotel in her red fur coat, no trace was left of that morning's visit, nor was there any sign of the old woman, the house appeared to be empty, the door beneath the sign GRAND HÔTEL MARÉCHAL LYAUTEY was slamming open and shut, she felt unreal, like a character in an old movie, wandering through an uninhabited wasteland with her pocketbook slung over her shoulder, carrying a suitcase, without any idea of where the road she was senselessly, stubbornly taking would lead, heading, against all common sense, in the direction the young Dane must have taken, toward the mountain with its attendant cloud, thinking of her conversation with

the logician, D., and of how she had formed an image of Tina von Lambert just for the sake of action, any kind of action, but now that this image had turned out to be a fiction, now that a banal marital problem had emerged in its place and revealed the fate of a completely different woman whom she had never heard of, but whose red fur coat she was wearing, the same coat Tina had worn, she felt herself transformed into this other woman, the Danish journalist Jytte Sörensen, and perhaps that had to do, mainly, with the Kierkegaard quote, for she too felt as helpless as a spider falling into empty space, this road she was taking now, dusty, stony, exposed to the pitiless sun, which had long broken through the cloud barrier that was boiling beneath it and twisting around the mountain slopes and squeezing through weirdly shaped rocks, this road was a consequence of her whole life, she had always acted spontaneously, the first time she had ever hesitated was when Otto von Lambert asked her to come to his house with her crew, and yet she had gone to see him and had accepted his assignment, and now she was walking along this road, reluctant and yet unable to do otherwise, carrying her suitcase like a hitch-hiker on a street without cars, until she was standing in front of Björn Olsen's naked corpse, so suddenly that she knocked against him with her foot, he lay before her, still laughing, it seemed, the way she had seen him at the foot of the stairs, completely covered with white dust, so that he looked more like a statue than a corpse, the corduroy pants, the jogging shoes, the padded jacket were scattered among the round tin film containers he had brought, most of them open, burst, rolls of film winding out of them like black intestines, and behind this mess the VW bus, torn apart from inside, a grotesque confusion of tin and steel, a bent and lacerated heap of scrap metal, machine parts, wheels, shards of glass, a sight that froze her to the spot, the corpse, the rolls of film, suitcases strewn about, some of them open, pieces of clothing, a pair of underpants flapping on a bent antenna like a flag—the details registered only gradually—, the ruined bus, the remains of the steering wheel still grasped by the Dane's severed hand, she saw all these things from where she stood before the corpse, and yet what she saw seemed unreal to her, something about it bothered her, made its reality unreal, a sound that suddenly came to her attention, but it had already been there when she had bumped against the corpse, and when she looked in the direction from which the quiet whirring came, she saw a tall, thin, lanky man in a dirty white linen suit, who was filming her, who waved to her and kept on filming, then limped over to her with his camera, laboriously lifting a leg to step over the corpse, then filmed it, standing next to her, as if to shoot it from her perspective, and as he did that he suggested she put down that dumb suitcase, limped over to the side, swung the camera over in her direction again, followed her, limping, as she retreated and sharply demanded to know what he wanted and who he was, for she had the impression the man was drunk, whereupon he let the camera sink and replied that people called him Polypheme, and that he no longer remembered what his name had been before that, it wasn't important anyway, the secret service had asked him to work as a cameraman for her, but he had declined, given the country's political situation it was too risky, working for her, whatever the police knew the secret service knew also, and whatever the secret service knew was known to the army, it was impossible to keep anything secret, he had chosen to secretly follow her instead, he knew what she was looking for, the head of the secret service had told all the cameramen in the country, and there were zillions of cameramen, that she, F., wanted to find and possibly catch the killer of the Danish woman, which was why she had put on her red fur coat, he for his part thought that was fantastic, eventually he would show her the films he had shot of her, not just since she had been deposited in that rubble heap, the Grand Hôtel Maréchal Lyautey, but earlier, when she found and bought the red fur coat in the blind man's stall in the old city, he had filmed that scene too, so had others probably, he wasn't the only one interested in her enterprise, even now she was being watched through telescope lenses from all sides, they could pierce through thick fog, all these explanations pouring like a torrent from the tall, lanky man, from this cavern full of rotting teeth, surrounded by white stubble, from a skinny, furrowed face with small burning eyes, from the face of a limping man in a dirt-smeared linen suit, standing with his legs spread over the corpse, F. filming again and again with a video camera, and when she asked him point-blank what he wanted, he answered: a deal, and when she asked what he meant by that, he explained that he had always admired her film portraits, it was his greatest desire to make a portrait of her, he had filmed the Danish woman, Sörensen, too, and since F. was interested in what had happened to her, he would offer her the films he had made of the Danish woman in exchange for the portrait he intended to make of F., he was in a position to convert the videocassettes into conventional films, the Sörensen woman had been on the trail of a secret, and now she, F., had a chance to pick up the scent and follow it further, he for his part was ready to go with her to an area in the desert where Sörensen had been, none of the people watching her now had ever dared go there, but she could trust him, he was known in certain circles as the most fearless of all cameramen, although these circles could not be named and his films could not be shown, for economic and political reasons which he would prefer not to divulge in the presence of the young Dane's corpse, it would be disrespectful, since he too was a victim of those self-same reasons.

‖ **16** ‖ He limped back to the bus without waiting for an answer, she was sure now that he was drunk, and when he had disappeared behind the bus, she knew she was about to make another mistake, but if she was going to find out what had happened to the Danish woman, she would have to trust this man, even though there was nothing trustworthy about him, this Polypheme who was apparently being watched just as she was, in fact how did she know they weren't watching her because they were watching him, she felt like a chess figure that was being pushed back and forth, and it was with some reluctance that she stepped over the dead body and walked around the ruined

bus, where she saw Polypheme at the wheel of
a Land-Rover, put her suitcase on the backseat
and sat down next to him, smelling an unmis-
takable whiff of whiskey as he suggested to her
that she buckle her seat belt, for the drive that
began now was infernal, dust clouds whirling behind them as they raced downhill along the mountain ridge, deep into the boiling cloud barrier,
sometimes so close to the edge of the road that
stones flew clattering into the ravines below them,
eventually down even steeper hairpin curves, once
in a while the drunk man would miss a turn and
drive the massive vehicle over the edge and down
the rocky slope, while F., tightly buckled to her
seat, her feet pressing against the front of the car,
could hardly see the mountain, or the savanna
they were plunging into and through which they
flew in the direction of the desert, startling jackals
and rabbits, snakes that shot away like arrows, and
other animals, into the stone desert, shrouded in
a black, cawing cloud, for hours, it seemed, then,
after leaving the birds behind, on and on through
harsh sunlight, until the Land-Rover abruptly
stopped, raising a cloud of dust, in front of a rather
flat heap of rubble in the middle of a plain that
looked like a Martian landscape, an impression
that was perhaps due to the light it exuded, for

it was covered with some peculiar substance, at once rocklike and rusty-metallic, and was ferociously punctured by huge, bent metal shapes, enormous steel splinters and thorns, which, by the time the dust cloud finally settled, F. had but a few seconds to look at, for the Land-Rover was already sinking beneath the ground, a roof closed over it, they were inside a subterranean garage, and when she asked where they were, he mumbled something she could not make out, an iron door slid open, and he limped ahead of her through several more iron doors that slid open as he approached them, through cellarlike rooms that also had the look of a photographer's studio, the walls densely covered with tiny photographs, as if for some absurd reason someone had spliced whole rolls of developed film into thousands of separate frames, several large pictures of destroyed armored cars in the midst of a wild mess of photography books strewn across various tables and chairs, also reams of scribbled sheets of paper, mountainous stacks of film rolls, metal racks from which strips of film were suspended, also baskets full of film scraps, then a photo lab, boxes full of dias, a projection room, a corridor, until, perpetually lurching and swaying on his injured leg, he led her into a windowless room whose walls were covered with photographs, with an art nouveau bed and a small table in the same style, a grotesque room with an adjoining toilet and shower, the guest apartment, as he put it, pronouncing the words with an effort, tottering against the wall of the corridor, and leaving F. by herself as she sullenly entered the room, but when she turned around, the door had shut behind her.

||| **17** ||| Only gradually did she become conscious of the fear that had seized her since she had entered this underground building, an insight that prompted her to do the most reasonable instead of the most unreasonable thing, to stop trying to open the door that could not be opened, to ignore her fear, to lie down on the art nouveau bed and try to figure out who this Polypheme might be, she had never heard of a cameraman with that nickname, nor could she imagine what this place was for, it must have been built at enormous cost, but by whom, and what was the meaning of the gigantic ruins outside, what was going on here and why this strange offer to swap his portrait of

Jytte Sörensen for a portrait of her, pondering these questions she fell asleep, and when she woke up suddenly, it seemed to her that the walls had shaken and the bed had danced, she must have dreamed it, inadvertently she began to look at the photographs, with growing horror, for they showed Björn Olsen being blown up in his car, the pictures must have been taken by a camera with a technical precision she could not even imagine, the first picture showing the outlines of the VW bus, the next one a small white sphere approximately where the clutch would be, then a gradual expansion of the sphere, the bus turning transparent and losing its shape, it was disintegrating, Olsen was being blasted off his seat, and the various phases looked particularly ghastly as Olsen, rising into the air, left one hand behind, severed from its arm, still holding the wheel, he seemed to be whistling gaily, she leaped out of bed, horrified, and instinctively moved toward the door, which, to her surprise, slid open, and, glad to be out of this room that felt to her like a prison cell, she stepped into the hallway, which was empty, stood still, suspecting a trap, heard someone hammering against an iron door somewhere, followed the sound, the doors sliding open as she approached them, walked hesitantly through the rooms she had already seen, found new corridors, bedrooms, technical labs with apparatuses she had never seen, this place must have been built for many people, where were they, with every step she felt more endangered, Polypheme must have left her alone for some devious reason, she was sure he was watching her, she came closer and closer to the hammering, now it seemed very near, now farther away, suddenly she stood at the end of a corridor in front of an iron door with a normal lock, a key inside the lock, and someone hammering against this door, sometimes it seemed as if someone were throwing himself against it, she was tempted to turn the key, but then it occurred to her that it might be Polypheme, he had been drunk and his manner of leaving her had been strange, some thought must have shot through his head, he had seemed to be staring through her, as if she weren't really there, he could have accidentally locked himself in by accident, the lock might have jammed, or a third person might have locked him in, the place was enormous, perhaps it wasn't as uninhabited as it seemed, and why did all the doors open automatically, the banging and hammering continued, she called, Polypheme, Polypheme, the answer was more banging and hammering, but maybe no sound carried through the iron door, but what if it wasn't a trap at all, maybe she wasn't being watched, maybe she was free, she ran back to her cell, didn't find it, ran along several passageways, entered a cell that at first she took to be hers but which wasn't, finally she found hers after all, slung her pocketbook over her shoulder, hurried back through the underground room, still hearing the hammering and banging, finally she found the garage door, it slid to the side, there was the Land-Rover, she sat down in the driver's seat, examined the dashboard, where, in addition to the usual instruments, she found two buttons with engraved arrows, one pointing up, one down, pressed the button with the arrow pointing up, the roof opened, the Land-Rover was lifted up, she was outside, above her the sky, and silhouetted against it, ruins, like sharp-pointed spears, long shadows cast by a bright, extinguishing spark, the earth jerking backward, the red stripe of light on the horizon began to narrow, she was in the closing jaws of a world-monster, and as she experienced the coming of night, the transformation of light into shadow and shadow into a darkness in which the stars were suddenly there, she experienced with certainty that freedom was the trap into which she was expected to flee, she let the Land-Rover float back down, the roof closed above her, the pounding and hammering had fallen silent, she ran back into her cell, and as she threw herself onto the bed, she felt something approaching, a howling, a thud, a bursting, far away and yet very near, a shivering, the bed and the table danced, she shut her eyes, she didn't know for how long, or whether she had fainted or not, she didn't care, and when she opened her eyes, Polypheme was standing before her.

||| **18** ||| He put her suitcase next to her bed,
he was sober, freshly shaved, and was wearing a
clean white suit and a black shirt, he said it was
half past ten, he'd been looking for her all over,
this wasn't her apartment, she'd obviously lost her
way, the earthquake last night must have scared
her, at any rate breakfast was ready and he'd be
waiting for her, and he limped out of the room,
the door shut behind him, she stood up, the bed
was a couch, the pictures on the walls showed the
successive stages of an exploding armored car, a
man caught in the tower was burning, blackening,
twisting, staring at the sky, she opened the suitcase,
got undressed, showered, put on a fresh denim

dress, opened the door, again the hammering and banging, then silence, she walked and lost her way, then some rooms she remembered, in one room a table swept clean of papers and photographs, bread, slices of corned beef on a board, tea, a jar full of water, a tin can, glasses, Polypheme came limping in from a corridor, an empty tin bowl in his hand, as if he had just finished feeding an animal, removed a stack of photography books from a chair, another stack from a second chair, they sat down, he used his pocketknife to cut the bread into slices and invited her to help herself, poured himself some tea, took a slice of bread, some corned beef, she suddenly felt hungry, he poured some white powder into a glass, poured water into it, in the morning he only drank powdered milk with water, he said, he was sorry about yesterday, he'd had too much to drink, was drinking too much altogether these days, revolting, this milk, that wasn't an earthquake, she said, no, it wasn't, he replied, pouring more water into his glass, adding that it would be unfair not to let her know the situation she'd unwittingly gotten herself into, because, he continued, apparently she had no idea what was actually going on in the country, and there was something sarcastic, superior about him, in fact he seemed completely different from the man she had met near the exploded VW bus, of course, he continued, she would know all about the power struggle between the police chief and the head of the secret service, the former was planning a coup d'etat and, naturally, the other was trying to prevent it, but there were other interests involved, the country she'd come to with such foolhardy naïveté did not just live off tourism and the conversion of vegetable matter into pillow stuffing, its principal source of revenue was a war with a neighboring country, a war for control of an area in the great sand desert that was uninhabited except for a few stray bedouins and desert fleas, where not even tourism had dared to set foot, a war that had been creeping along for ten years now and no longer served any purpose except to test the products of all the weapons-exporting countries, it wasn't just French, German, English, Italian, Swedish, Israeli, and Swiss tanks fighting against Russian and Czech tanks, but also Russian against Russian machinery, American against American, German against German, Swiss against Swiss, the desert was peppered with the wreckage of tank battles, the war effort was constantly seeking out new battlefields, quite logically, since the stability of the market depended on weapons exports, provided these weapons were truly competitive, real wars were constantly breaking out, like the one between Iran and Iraq, for instance, no need to mention others, where the testing of weapons came just a bit late, and that was the reason, he said, why the weapons industry was so committed to this insignificant war, which had long lost its political meaning, it was a make-believe war, the instructors of the weapons-exporting industrial nations were almost exclusively training local people, Berbers, Moors, Arabs, Jews, blacks, poor devils who had attained some privilege thanks to this war and could now get by, more or less, but there was unrest in the country, the fundamentalists regarded the war as a criminal plot on the part of the West, which was true if one included the Warsaw Pact, the head of the secret service was trying to turn the war into an international scandal, and the Sörensen case was just grist for the mill, the government, too, would like to stop the war, if only they weren't faced with economic disaster, the head of the general staff was still vacillating, the Saudis were undecided, the police chief wanted the war to continue, he was bribed by the weapons-producing countries and also, according to rumor, by both the Israelis and Iran, and was trying to overthrow the government, supported by otherwise unemployed cameramen and photographers from every corner of the globe, this war was their bread and butter because its only meaning resided in the fact that it could be observed, it was the only way to test the weapons and correct their faults, and as for himself—he laughed, took some more powdered milk and water (she had long since finished her breakfast)—well, that was a slightly more involved business, everyone had his story, she had hers, he had his, he had no idea how hers had begun, nor did he want to know, but as for his own story, it had begun on a Monday evening in the Bronx, his father had run a small photography studio, pictures of weddings and of anyone who wanted his picture taken, and one day he unwittingly put a picture of a gentleman in his shopwindow which shouldn't have been put there, a fact that was brought to his attention by a member of the gang, with a submachine gun, so that his father's perforated body had fallen on top of him, for he had been sitting on the ground behind the counter bent over his homework, in short it all started that Monday evening, for his father had been determined to give his son a higher education, fathers' hopes for their sons always aim much too high, but when he crawled out from under his father after a while, since the shooting had stopped, he understood, looking around the wrecked store, that real education consisted of knowing how to get ahead in the world by using the world one wants to get ahead in, and so, with the only camera that had not been destroyed by the shooting, he descended into the underworld, little shrimp that he was, his first specialty was the pickpockets, the police didn't pay much for his snapshots and made few arrests, which was why he went undetected for so long, whereupon he grew bolder and started photographing burglars with equipment that was partly stolen, partly built out of old bits and pieces, he was living with the intelligence of a rat, because in order to photograph burglars you had to think like a burglar, they lived by their wits and avoided the light, a few cat burglars had fallen off fire escapes, blinded by his flashbulb, he still felt sorry for them, but the police had continued to pay poorly, and taking his pictures to the press would have alarmed the underworld, so he had been lucky, no one had suspected a photographer in this skinny little urchin, and he got too big for his britches, tried his luck with killers, never giving a thought to the kind of danger he was exposing himself to, and now the police paid handsomely, one killer after the other either went to the electric chair or was knocked off by his boss for security reasons, but one day in Central Park he took a snapshot, purely by accident, and ruined a senator's career, setting loose an avalanche of scandals that forced the police to reveal his previously unknown identity to a congressional committee, the FBI ferreted him out, the committee took him apart, and, his picture in all the papers, he returned to New York and found his studio in the same condition his father's store had been in, he'd kept his head above water for a while by selling the cops pictures of killers and selling the killers pictures of detectives, but after a while everyone was chasing him, cops and killers alike, and his only recourse had been to take shelter in the army, they needed photographers too, legal and illegal ones, but, he reflected, leaning back in his armchair and putting his feet on the table, "taking shelter" was kind of exaggerated, wars weren't exactly popular, not even when they were dressed up as administrative measures, delegates and senators, diplomats and journalists had to be persuaded, and if they couldn't be persuaded, they had to be blackmailed, for which purpose he was given access to luxury whorehouses, the pictures he shot there were political dynamite, he'd been forced to do it, the army could have sent him home anytime, and in view of the fate that waited for him there, he had done what they wanted, and done it so well that, as another congressional committee was about to convene, he fled from the army to the air force, and from there, since no one was as stubborn as a vengeful politician, to the weapons industry, where everyone's interests converged, a solid hope of security at last, and that was how he had landed here, bruised and battered, a perpetually hunted hunter, a legendary figure for the insiders in his profession, which was why they elected him to be their boss, and he had accepted, one of the most harebrained decisions he had ever made, for now he was the head of an illegal organization that supplied information about all the weapons that were being used and whose purpose could be defined as that of making espionage obsolete, if anyone wanted to find out about an enemy tank or the effectiveness of an antitank cannon, he was their man, it was thanks to him the war hadn't petered out altogether, and yet, on account of his all too powerful position, the administration had taken a renewed interest in him, they'd approached him with a plan to destroy the organization, saying he was the major expert in his field and they weren't trying to force him, but certain senators— very well, he had accepted their assignment and now the organization was beginning to crumble, it was questionable whether the war could continue, and as for his former colleagues, that they should search for him now, and watch him intently wherever he showed up, was only natural, all the more so since, admittedly, he had kept certain excessively subtle information to himself.

||| **19** ||| He fell silent, he had talked and talked and she had sensed that he had to talk, that he was telling her things he may never have told anyone, but she also sensed that there was something he wasn't telling her and that what he wasn't telling her was part of the reason why he was telling her the story of his life, he sat there leaning back in his chair, his legs on the table, staring into space as if waiting for something, and there was another howling, another thud, a bursting, a trickling of plaster, then silence, she asked him what that was, he replied, it's the reason why no one dares come here, limped to the laboratory, a stairway descended from above, they climbed

up and entered a small room with a shallow-domed
ceiling that vaulted across a solid row of small
windows, but not until she was sitting next to him
did she notice that the windows were monitors,
one of which showed the sun setting and the floor
of the desert opening up, the Land-Rover rising,
herself sitting in the Land-Rover, then she saw
the reddish-yellow stripe narrow and vanish, the
sudden nightfall, the Land-Rover sinking, the stars
breaking through, something flying, a bright light,
the monitor blacked out, now the same thing again
in super-slow motion now, he said, night descending
in shifts and jerks, the Land-Rover sinking bit by bit,
the stars lighting up in spasms, one of them growing, cometlike, bit by bit, a slender, brilliant white
shape drilling itself into the desert, staccato, and
slowly exploding by shifts and starts, casting debris
into the air, volcanolike, gradually, then only light,
darkness, that was the first one, he said, the second
one had exploded nearer by, their precision was
increasing, and when F. asked what all this was
about, Polypheme replied, an intercontinental
missile, and a picture of the desert appeared in
another monitor, the mountains, the city too, the
desert came nearer, a cross appeared over the picture, there, he said, that was where F. and he were,
the picture came from a satellite whose orbit was

so perfectly adjusted to the rotation of the earth that it was always floating above them, and he activated another monitor, the whole thing's automated, he said, the desert again, a small black square by the left margin, the Al-Hakim ruin, the city on the top right, the mountain by the left margin, the cloud was still there, a blinding white cotton ball, at the center of the picture a small sphere with antennas, the first satellite as observed by a second satellite for the purpose of observing what it was observing, at which point he turned off the monitors, limped to the stairs, walked down without paying her any attention, went back to the room, to the table, picked up some corned beef with his hands, sat down, leaned back, put his feet on the table, said the next one was on its way, ate, and explained as he ate that while modern conventional weapons were tested in the desert, the strategic conceptions of both sides required a careful inspection of the target precision of intercontinental, continental, and submarine-based missiles, of the functional capacity of these weapons systems that served as vehicles for the atom and hydrogen bombs, preserving world peace at the risk of killing both peace and the world, either by relying too heavily on the intimidation of the enemy or on the computer or on an ideology or even on

God, since the enemy could lose his head, the computer could make mistakes, an ideology could be wrong, and God could turn out to be uninterested, and, on the other hand, ignoring the fact that those powers that were solely equipped with conventional weapons and ought to duck low were sorely tempted to take advantage of world peace and wage conventional wars in the shadow of deterrence, for given the possibility of nuclear war, conventional wars had become quite acceptable, giving renewed impetus to the production of conventional weapons and justifying the war in the desert, a perfect cycle, brilliantly designed to keep the weapons industry and therefore the world economy productive and happy, the function of this station, he said, was to speed up the process, it had been made possible by a secret treaty and had been built at fantastic expense, the observation center's electronic system, for example, was fed through underground cables by a dam and a power plant that had been especially constructed in the mountains, it wasn't by chance that this part of the desert was chosen as a target field and that half a million dollars were spent on it each year, it was fairly close to those oil-rich countries that were constantly yielding to the temptation to blackmail the industrial nations, the observation center had been equipped with over fifty specialists, all of them technicians, he was the only cameraman among them, still working with his father's old Kodak for the most part, he had only recently started fiddling with video, he had never gone to the observation center, no matter how big a missile was predicted, he had managed to take some sensational shots, admittedly a bomb fragment had smashed his leg, but when he was finally stitched together and came back, he found the observation center half abandoned, it had been fully automated, the technicians who were still there were working with computers, he really wasn't needed anymore, he had been replaced by fully automated video cameras, then a satellite had been launched to a permanent position above the observation center, they weren't informed that the observation center for the satellite was in the Canaries, a television specialist discovered the satellite purely by accident, and later the second one, then that one was spotted by the other side, shortly after that came the order to evacuate the station because it was now capable of functioning fully automatically, which was a lie, what the hell was the satellite for, he alone, Polypheme, had stayed, he didn't know anything about all these installations, all he could do, barely, was check to see whether the videos were still working, and they were, but for how long, the place was being powered by batteries now, the supply from the power plant had been turned off that morning, once the batteries were exhausted the observation center was useless, and now they'd started to fix up the intercontinental missiles with not quite nuclear but very fancy conventional bombs, and though it seemed farfetched to assume that both sides were aiming not so much at the station as at him, because he was in possession of various films and negatives that might prove more than embarrassing for certain diplomats, he had taken to drink, he never used to drink, whereupon F. asked him whether these documents that were in his possession were the reason why he had killed Björn Olsen.

‖ 20 ‖ He removed his feet from the table, stood up, pulled a bottle of whiskey out from among the rolls of film, poured some whiskey into the glass from which he had drunk the powdered milk, swirled it, drank all of it, asked her whether she believed in God, poured himself another whiskey, and sat down again, facing her, she was confused by his question, which at first she wanted to dismiss with impatience, but then, sensing that she would find out more about him if she took his question seriously, she replied that she could no longer believe in a god, because, on the one hand, she did not know what sort of god concept she was supposed to have, and how could she believe in something she couldn't conceive of, and on the other hand she had no idea what he, who was asking her about her beliefs, might mean when he spoke of a god in whom she was supposed to believe or not believe, to which he replied that if there was a god, a purely spiritual being, it would have to consist of pure observation and be incapable of intervening in the evolutionary unfolding of the material process—which culminates in nothingness, he said, since even protons eventually disintegrate, and in the course of which the earth, plants, animals, and people evolve and pass away— so, only if God were a pure observer could he remain unsullied by his creation, and this applied to himself as a cameraman as well, since his job consisted of pure observation, and if that weren't the case he would long since have put a bullet through his brain, any emotion such as fear, love, pity, anger, contempt, revenge, guilt, not only dulled pure perception but made it impossible, tainted it with feeling, left it contaminated with this disgusting world instead of lifted above it, reality could only be objectively comprehended by means of a camera, aseptically, the camera alone was capable of capturing the space and time within which experience took place, while without a camera, experience slid off into nothingness, since the moment something was experienced it had already passed and was therefore just a memory and, like all memory, falsified, fictive, which was why it sometimes seemed to him that he was no longer human—since being human required the illusion of being able to experience something directly—, and that he was really like the cyclops Polypheme, who experienced the world through a single round hole in the middle of his forehead as if through a camera, and therefore he had not only blown up the VW bus to prevent Olsen from continuing to investigate the fate of the Danish woman journalist and ending up in the position she, F., now found herself in, his main objective, he added, after another whining howl and thud and bursting crash and shivering reverberation (farther away now, and gentler), and after a casual "not even close this time," his main objective had been to film the explosion, however she shouldn't get him wrong, a terrible misfortune, no question, but thanks to the camera the event had been immortalized, a metaphor of global catastrophe, because the purpose of a camera was to arrest time, a tenth, a hundredth, even a thousandth of a second, to stop time by destroying time, film, too, he said, only seemed to reproduce reality when it was run through a projector, it created the illusion of process when actually it consisted of successive still shots, so when he made a film, he would splice the roll into all its separate components, each one of them a crystallized reality, an infinitely precious thing, but now the two satellites were hovering above him, there was time when he had felt like a god with his camera, but now everything he observed was observed from above, and not only what he observed, he himself was being observed as he observed, he knew the resolving power of satellite pictures, a god who was observed was no longer a god, God was not subject to observation, God's freedom consisted in being a concealed, hidden god, while man's bondage consisted of being observed, but what was even worse was the nature of those who observed and made a fool of him, namely a system of computers, for what was observing was two cameras connected to two computers observed by two further computers and fed into computers connected to *those* computers in order to be scanned, converted, reconverted, and, after further processing by laboratory computers, developed, enlarged, viewed, and interpreted, by whom and where and whether at any point by human beings, he couldn't tell, computers could be programmed to recognize details and register irregularities in satellite pictures, he, Polypheme, was a fallen god, his place had been taken by a computer who was being watched by a second computer, one god was watching another, the world was spinning back to its origin.

||| 21 ||| He had drunk one glass of whiskey after another, only occasionally adding a bit of water, he had also turned back into the man she had met near the disfigured corpse of the Dane, an alcoholic with a furrowed face and small burning eyes that nevertheless appeared petrified, as if they had stared into some cold horror throughout eternity, and when she asked, haphazardly, whose idea it had been to call him Polypheme, she sat back, for she had scarcely uttered the question when he put the bottle to his lips and then replied, with a thick tongue, that she had twice been in danger of death, once when she went outside and the rockets came, and earlier, in front of the iron gate,

if she had opened it she would be dead now, for the name Polypheme had been given him on the aircraft carrier *Kitty Hawk*, at a time when the withdrawal from North Vietnam had already been decided on, in the cabin he had shared with a red-haired giant, a strange bird, a professor of Greek at some hillbilly university who read Homer while he was off duty, the *Iliad*, reciting the verses out loud, one hell of a bomber pilot, too, nicknamed Achilles, partly to make fun of him for being different, partly out of respect for his enormous courage, a loner whom he had photographed and filmed many times, the best work he had ever done, for Achilles never paid him any attention, never exchanged more than a few casual words with him, until, several hours before they were to carry out a night raid on Hanoi in a new type of bomber, an assignment that both of them had a presentiment would fail, Achilles looked up from his Homer, saw the camera pointed at him, and said, you are Polypheme, and laughed, the only time he had ever laughed, and the last time too, and then he started talking, and that, too, was the first time, saying the Greeks had distinguished between Ares, the god of war and bloodshed, and Athena, the goddess of military operations, in hand-to-hand combat it was dangerous to think ahead, all one could do was react with lightning speed, thrust and parry, evade a flung spear, ward off a swung sword, strike, stab, facing the enemy, body to body, his rage, his gasps, his sweat and blood mixing with one's own rage, one's own gasps, one's own sweat, one's own blood in a wild knot of fear and hate, a clawing and biting of man against man, a ripping and chopping and cutting, men turned to beasts tearing other beasts to pieces, that was how Achilles had fought at Troy, with murderous, hateful passion, roaring with rage, rejoicing at every enemy's death, but as for himself, who was also called Achilles, how humiliating, as war became more and more technical, the enemy had become more and more abstract, a barely perceptible target for the marksman aiming through a telescopic sight, a subject of pure surmise for the artillery, and as a bomber pilot, he could, if pressed, indicate how many cities and villages he had bombarded, but not how many people he had killed, nor how he had killed and mangled and squashed and burned them, he didn't know, he just watched his instruments and followed his wireless operator's instructions, coordinating his speed and the direction of the wind, until the plane had arrived at that abstract point in the stereometric grid of longitude, latitude, and altitude, then the automatic discharge of bombs, and after the attack he did not feel himself a hero but a coward, there was a dark suspicion in him sometimes that an SS henchman at Auschwitz had behaved more morally than he, because he had been confronted with his victims, even though he regarded them as subhuman trash, while between himself and his victims no confrontation took place, the victims weren't even subhuman, just an unspecified something, it wasn't very different from exterminating insects, the pilot spraying the vines from his plane couldn't see the mosquitoes either, and no matter what you called it, bombing, destroying, liquidating, pacifying, it was abstract, mechanical, and could only be understood as a sum, probably a financial sum, one dead Vietnamese was worth more than a hundred thousand dollars, morality was expunged like an evil tumor, hate was injected as a stimulant against an enemy who was a phantom, whenever he saw a real captured enemy he wasn't able to hate him, true, he was fighting against a system he found politically unacceptable, but every system, even the most criminal, was made up of guilty and innocent members, and in every system, including the war machine he was serving, crime entered in, overgrew and stifled the cause, he felt like a nonentity, a mere observer of dials and clocks, and

especially in this night raid they were being sent
out on, their plane was a flying computer, programmed to start, fly to the target, drop its bombs,
all automatic, their only function was to observe,
he sometimes wished he could be a real criminal,
do something inhuman, be a beast, rape and
strangle a woman, the idea of a human being was
an illusion, man either became a soulless machine,
a camera, a computer, or a beast, and after this
speech, the longest Achilles had ever held forth,
he had fallen silent and a few hours later they
had both flown at low altitude at twice the speed
of sound toward Hanoi, toward the fire-spewing
gorge of anti-aircraft guns, the CIA had warned
Hanoi, a test required an adequate defense, nevertheless he had managed to take some of his best
photographs, then their plane had been hit, they
had already dropped the bombs, the automatic
pilot had fallen out, Achilles had steered the
heavily damaged plane back to the *Kitty Hawk*,
streams of blood flowing from a wound in his head,
seeming less like a person now than a computer,
for when they had landed and the machine had
come to a standstill, the bloody and vacant face
of an idiot had gaped at him, he had never been
able to forget Achilles, he would remain indebted
to him for the rest of his life, he had read the

*Iliad* in order to understand this hillbilly professor who had saved his life and had become an idiot for his sake, he had searched for Achilles, but it was years before he had found him in the psychiatric department of the military hospital where his, Polypheme's, leg was treated, he had found an idiot god who had been locked up in a cell because he had escaped from the ward several times and raped and killed women, whereupon he fell silent and stared into space again, and, when F. asked whether the creature behind the door was Achilles, he replied that she must understand, he had to fulfill the only desire it was still capable of feeling, and besides, he had promised to give her the portrait of Jytte Sörensen.

||| **22** ||| After a long search for a roll of film, he had difficulty getting the projector to start, but finally, leaning back in a movie seat, her legs crossed, she saw Jytte Sörensen for the first time, a slender woman in a red fur coat walking in the desert, at first F. thought it was a film of herself, but then she noticed that whenever the woman stopped, something forced her to move on, she never saw her face, but she could tell by the shadow that appeared from time to time that Polypheme's Land-Rover was forcing her into the desert, Jytte Sörensen walked and walked, stone desert, sand desert, but it was not an aimless wandering, even though she was being forced, for F.

had the feeling that the Danish woman was trying to reach a specific place, but suddenly she ran down a steep slope, fell head over heels, the Al-Hakim ruin came into view with the holy men squatting like black birds, she got up, she ran toward them, hugged the knees of the first man she reached, wanted to beg for help, he keeled over, just like the man F. had pushed, the woman crawled over the corpse, embraced the knees of the second holy man, he too was a corpse, the shadow of the vehicle appeared, black as tar, then a huge creature threw himself on her suddenly slack and un-resisting body and raped and killed her, everything shown with exaggerated precision, a close-up of her face, for the first time, then the face of the creature, moaning, greedy, fleshy, vacant, what followed then must have been shot with a special camera, for it was night, the woman's body lay among the holy men, the two corpses were sitting upright again, jackals came, sniffed, began to eat Jytte Sörensen, and only now did F. notice that she was alone in the projection room, she stood up, left the projection room, stopped, took a cigarette out of her pocketbook, lit it, smoked, Polypheme was sitting at the table, splicing a strip of film, next to him a metal stand with film cuttings, on the table a revolver next to several pictures he had cut

out of the filmstrips, at the end of the table a
bald-headed man who was scanning verses, Greek
hexameters, Homer, swaying back and forth to the
beat, eyes closed, and Polypheme said he had
stuffed him full of Valium, then, cutting out another picture, he asked her what she thought of his
material, a video converted to 16-millimeter film,
she did not know how to answer, he looked at her,
indifferent, cold, what you call reality, she said, is
staged, whereupon he, examining the frame he
had cut out, replied that only plays could be staged,
not reality, he had made Sörensen visible, just as
a space probe had made the active volcanoes of one
of Jupiter's moons visible, to which she replied,
that's sophistic, and he, reality is not sophistic,
and then, after another detonation followed by a
drizzle of plaster, she wanted to know why he
had called Achilles an idiot god, to which he replied that he called him that because Achilles behaved like a god who had become infected with
his creation, a god who destroyed his creatures,
but that woman, she interjected angrily, that
woman was not the idiot's creation, so much the
worse for God, he replied calmly, and, asked
whether it was supposed to happen here, he said no,
not next to the Al-Hakim ruin either, it could be
observed by satellite, the portrait of the Danish

woman was faulty, but the portrait of F. would be a masterpiece, he had already picked the place, and now she should leave him and Achilles alone, he had to pack his things, they would be leaving at night, he would take her and also the films and photos for which he was being hunted, he was leaving the station forever, whereupon he went back to splicing the filmstrip, while she, suddenly filled with such deadly indifference that she was not even conscious of obeying him, returned to her cell and lay down on the art nouveau bed or the couch, she didn't care, for it was impossible to flee, he had become sober again and was armed, Achilles could wake up, and again and again the building was shaken, and even if she had intended to flee, she was not sure whether she wanted to, she saw Jytte Sörensen's face before her, a twisted grimace of lust, and then, for a moment, as the huge hands wrapped themselves around her throat, her features looked proud, triumphant, willing, the Danish woman had wanted it all, her rape and her death, everything else had been but a pretext, and she, she had to walk the path she had chosen to the end, for the sake of her choice, for the sake of her pride, for her own sake, a ridiculous and nevertheless implacable vicious circle of duty, but it was the truth she was seeking, the truth about herself, she thought of her encounter with von Lambert, she had accepted his assignment against her instinct, she had escaped from a vague plan into one that was even vaguer, just for the sake of action, because she was in the midst of a crisis, she thought of her conversation with D., he had been too polite to suggest that she give up her plan and perhaps too curious how things would turn out, von Lambert could send out another helicopter now, he was guilty all over again, she thought, and had to laugh, then she saw herself in the artist's studio, in front of the portrait, it was in fact a picture of Jytte Sörensen, but she had turned around too late, it must have been Tina who had left the room, and no doubt the director was her lover, she had been close to the truth but hadn't followed it up, the temptation to fly to M. had been too great, but even that flight may have been just a running away, but running from whom, she asked herself, from herself, possibly, perhaps she couldn't stand herself and the flight consisted of letting herself drift, she saw herself as a girl, standing by a mountain stream before it threw itself over the edge of a cliff, she had walked away from the camp and placed a small paper boat in the stream, and followed it, watched it getting caught by various stones and drifting loose again, and now

it was sailing inexorably toward the waterfall, and
the little girl watched with tremendous excitement
and pleasure, for she had put all her friends in the
ship, her sister, too, and her mother and father
and the freckled boy in her class who eventually
died of polio, she had put all the people she loved
in that boat, and as it began to shoot along like
an arrow, as it flew over the edge and down into
the abyss, she shouted with joy, and suddenly the
boat turned into a ship and the stream became a
river that was flowing toward a cataract, and she
was sitting in the ship that was drifting along
faster and faster, toward the waterfall, and above
it, on top of two cliffs, squatted Polypheme, holding a camera to his eye, and Achilles, who was
laughing and bouncing his naked torso up and
down.

║ 23 ║ They left shortly after a detonation that was so violent she thought the station was going to collapse, nothing was working right, the Land-Rover had to be lifted manually with a lever, and when they were finally outside, Polypheme handcuffed her to a bar on the backseat, where she lay among mountains of film rolls, he started the car and raced off, but there were no more rockets, they drove undisturbed, deeper and deeper south, above her the stars, whose names she had forgotten, except for one, Canopus, the star D. had told her she would be able to see, but now she didn't know if she saw it or not, and that filled her with a strange anguish, for she felt that Canopus would help her if she could only recognize it, then the stars began to pale, until just one was left, perhaps that was Canopus, the icy silvering of night into day, she was freezing, the sun rose, a great ball, Polypheme released her, and now he was herding her along in her red fur coat, through a pockmarked moon landscape of sand and stone, along wadis, past sand dunes and grotesque rock formations, into a hell of light and shadow, dust and dryness, exactly the way Jytte Sörensen had been herded through the desert, and behind her, almost touching her, now farther away, now nearly inaudible, now roaring toward her again, a monster playing with its victim, the Land-Rover, steered by Polypheme, next to him Achilles, still half stunned, swaying from side to side, reciting the *Iliad*, all that was left of his mind by the fragment of steel that had hit him, but Polypheme did not need to steer her, she walked and walked, wrapped in her fur coat, ran toward the sun, which was rising higher and higher, then a laugh behind her, the Land-Rover chased her the way the policeman in the white turban had chased the jackal, perhaps she was that jackal, she stopped, so did the Land-Rover, she was drenched with sweat, she took off her clothes, not caring that she was being watched, keeping only the fur coat on, and continued walking, the Land-Rover behind her, she walked and walked, the sun was burning away the sky, when the Land-Rover stopped and stayed behind, she heard the whirring of a camera, and here it was now, the attempted portrait of a murdered woman, except it was she who was going to be murdered, and it wasn't she who was making the portrait, she was being portrayed, and she wondered what would be done with her portrait, whether Polypheme would show it to other victims the way he had shown her the portrait of the Danish woman, then she stopped thinking, because it was senseless to think of anything, in the wavering distance she could see bizarre squat rocks, maybe a mirage, she thought, she had always wanted to see a mirage, but as she approached them, already staggering, the rocks turned out to be a tank cemetery, burned-out hulks standing around her like huge turtles, the mighty masts of searchlights that had once illuminated the battlefield stabbing the glittering void, but hardly had she recognized the place to which she had been herded when the shadow of the approaching Land-Rover fell over her like a cloak, and as Achilles stood before her, half naked, covered with dust, as if he had just come out of the thick of battle, his old khaki trousers torn, his naked feet encrusted with sand, his idiot's eyes wide open, she was seized by the enormous impact of the present and by a feeling she had never known, a desire to live, to live forever, to throw herself upon this giant, this idiot god, to sink her teeth into his throat, to change into a savage beast, devoid of all humanity, at one with him who wanted to rape and kill her, at one with the horrible stupidity of the world, but he seemed to evade her, turned in a circle, without her understanding why he evaded her, why he turned in a circle, fell, stood up again, stared at the American, German, French, Russian, Czech, Israeli, Swiss, Italian steel corpses, from which life began to stir, bodies climbing from rusted tanks and shattered scout cars, cameramen with their equipment, like fantastic animals, silhouetted against the burning silver of the sky, the head of the secret service crawled out of the dented ruins of a Russian SU 100, and, like milk boiling over the edge of a pot, the chief of police emerged from the command turret of a burned-out Centurion, each one had observed Polypheme and each had observed all the others, and as cameramen held up their cameras, standing on top of tanks and tank turrets and tank tracks, and the sound technicians raised their gear high and across, Achilles, hit by a second bullet, attacked one tank after another in impotent rage, and staggered backward, kicked from all sides, fell on his back again and again, writhed, heaved himself back to his feet, ran, choking, toward the Land-Rover, both hands pressed to his chest, blood running between his fingers, was struck by a third bullet, fell on his back again, roaring verses from the *Iliad* at Polypheme, who was filming him, raised himself to his feet once more, was perforated by a machine-gun salvo, fell back again, and died, whereupon Polypheme, while the others filmed him and each other, drove the Land-Rover in a curve around the ruined tanks and raced away, leaving behind the cars that pursued him, who needed only to follow his tracks, but that too was senseless, for when, toward midnight, they had come within a few miles of the observation center, an explosion shook the desert like an earthquake and a ball of fire rose to the sky.

||| **24** ||| Weeks later, after returning with her crew and after the television studios had rejected her film without any explanation, F. sat in the Italian restaurant listening to the logician D. reading a report in the morning paper about the execution of the head of the secret service and the chief of police on the orders of the head of state, the former chief of the general staff, who had accused them, respectively, of high treason and attempting to overthrow the government and had now flown south to inspect the troops he kept stationed there, evidently in order to continue the border dispute with his neighbor, after denying the rumors according to which a part of the desert was being used

as a target for foreign missiles, insisting on his country's neutrality, a report F. found especially amusing after D. read another account, on the opposite page, of the birth of a healthy baby boy to Otto and Tina von Lambert, the fulfillment of a long-cherished wish for the well-known psychiatrist and his wife, who had once been thought dead and buried, whereupon D., folding the newspaper, said to F., goddamn, were you lucky.

*Friedrich Dürrenmatt*
April 6, 1986